'I just wondered, boys,' said Dad, 'if you would

MAL

My Parents Are Driving Me Crazy

Pete Johnson

AWARD PUBLICATIONS LIMITED

ISBN 978-1-78270-160-6

First published by Award Publications Limited 2015

Published by Award Publications Limited,
The Old Riding School, The Welbeck Estate,
Worksop, Nottinghamshire, S80 3LR

www.awardpublications.co.uk

15 1

Printed in the United Kingdom

To my niece, Zoe,
who wishes Louis went to her school.

Chapter One

Dad Acts Like a Big Poo

Monday November 18th

4.30 p.m.
My bedroom walls have been invaded – by Post-It notes. Dead rude stuff too, like ...

LOUIS, WHY SHOULD I MAKE YOUR BED TODAY?
HOW LONG WOULD IT TAKE YOU TO DO IT?

LOUIS, DON'T LEAVE ALL THAT MESS ON THE
FLOOR FOR ME TO CLEAN UP, DO IT YOURSELF.

LOUIS, ALWAYS TAKE YOUR MUGS DOWNSTAIRS.
DON'T JUST LEAVE THEM ON THE WINDOW SILL

FOR ME TO DEAL WITH.

'Dad's done exactly the same in my room,' wailed Elliot, my midget brother. 'So it's like it's not my bedroom any more.'

Now Mum had often dropped into my bedroom to do a spot of cleaning. And I'd never minded. In fact, I was happy to let her tidy up my room whenever she wished.

But then Dad lost his job and Mum was offered a full-time post at the estate agents. So they decided to do a swap.

This is Dad's very first day as a stay-at-home dad. Well, he's got off to a truly terrible start. Can you believe he didn't even bother to carry my dirty mugs downstairs? Talk about lazy. He'd just grumped about, bunging up snotty notes everywhere.

'When I saw my bedroom, I was so mad,' said Elliot, 'I marched downstairs and shouted, "Dad, you're acting like a big poo!"'

'You didn't?'

'Well, I wanted to, but I thought I'd wait for you.'

I nodded and said, 'It can't be healthy for our impressionable young minds to be exposed to all this bossiness. Really, Dad's very lucky I didn't call *Childline*. But he has to be stopped: and he will be – after I've cleared up my room.'

Elliot looked shocked.

'No, the Post-it Notes must be obeyed.' Then in one mighty movement I picked up the mountains of stuff on the floor and hurled it all under my bed. Elliot giggled. Next I dashed about ripping down every one of Dad's notes and threw them under the bed too.

Elliot was falling about laughing now.

'Right, now for Dad,' I said.

'Yeah, let's sort him out,' said Elliot eagerly.

We marched downstairs together.

Dad was hoovering in a revoltingly, enthusiastic way, really ramming the hoover into every corner. But when he saw us he switched the hoover off and said, 'Hoovering is more tiring than it looks, you know. Good fun, though. So how's everything going?'

'Very badly,' I said. And Elliot and I stood grave-faced either side of him.

'Now, what can be wrong?' said Dad, grinning away. He'd been in a wildly, cheerful mood since first thing this morning when he'd gone on and on about how lucky he was to be escaping the daily grind. I hated to burst his bubble. But things had to be said.

'How would you like it, Dad,' I asked, 'if I stuck up notes all over your bedroom?'

'But I'm not asking you to clean *my* bedroom,' he replied. 'And I only put up a few friendly suggestions ...'

'Friendly ...?' Elliot and I echoed disbelievingly.

'I just wondered, boys,' said Dad, 'if you'd like to make more of a contribution to cleaning your rooms.'

I considered for a second. 'No, we wouldn't.'

'Ah, but this is where it gets interesting,' he said.

'I doubt that,' I muttered.

'Up to now, you haven't had the right kit.'

'Dad, we're not in the army,' I said.

'But now you have.' That's when he handed us both giant green dusters, the size of pillowcases. 'These are your very own dusters to keep,' he beamed.

'Really,' I muttered.

'Oh yes, I went out and got them for you specially.'

Some dads shower their sons with computer games, comics and tickets for football games – my dad buys us dusters.

'So, nothing to stop you getting stuck in now,' he grinned.

'Mum never asked us to do any dusting,' said Elliot.

'But now your mum has joined the full-time

workforce, so I'm in charge of the house – and I will be doing things a little differently to her. And I've decided that keeping your bedrooms clean and tidy will be your own personal responsibility. However I shall always be available to help and advise you.'

'You're spoiling us,' I muttered.

'I think we're going to make a great team,' he said.

After he charged back to his hoovering Elliot glared down at the unfamiliar object in his hand. 'What are we going to do with this?'

'Lose it as soon as possible. Don't worry, he'll have forgotten all about it in a couple of days,' I said.

7.05 p.m.

Normally Dad would stagger home about six o'clock and then sink down on the sofa, the laptop balanced on his knees, still doing stuff for work. And after he'd eaten, he'd fall asleep in front of the telly, usually with his mouth wide open.

But tonight he was shuffling about in his slippers making Mum a cup of tea. Mum couldn't crash out on the sofa, though, or even talk about her day. She was too busy wandering around admiring all the things Dad had done today.

11

'Boys, just look at these clean windows,' she called.

'OK, we're looking at them,' I said. 'Now what happens.'

Then Mum sat down in the kitchen saying how lovely it was to have a meal cooked for her for a change!

'Well, from now on, the kitchen is my domain, my little kingdom,' announced Dad. 'You are to leave everything to me, Jessica, all right?'

'You won't get any argument from me,' said Mum.

Then Dad brought in his vegetarian stew and handed round generous portions. 'Just tuck in,' he said. 'I've made enough for seconds.'

'Eeugh,' shouted Elliot, spraying his first mouthful right across the table.

'I should have brought an umbrella,' I quipped.

'Elliot, that is no way to behave at the table,' said Mum.

'But it's disgu—' he began.

'Not another word,' interrupted Mum fiercely.

'I don't think I got the flavour quite right,' said Dad.

'What flavour?' I murmured to Elliot. It didn't taste of anything except stale socks.

'Eat up, boys,' said Mum. 'It's wonderfully filling.'

Elliot whispered to me, 'I'd rather eat my own bogies than any more of Dad's stew.'

'You know what,' I whispered back, 'I think I'd rather eat your bogies too.'

7.15 p.m.
'I'd sack Dad,' Elliot has just announced to me.

'After one day?'

'Yeah, he's rubbish. I knew he would be. Dads are just not meant to be mums.'

Chapter Two

Early-Morning Fire

7.35 p.m.
Spent a ton of time – a whole twenty minutes – trying to write my history essay. But now my arm is aching and so is my brain. And I had to stop for the sake of my health.

The trouble is, this essay is already late, you know. Even worse, my history teacher is also the deputy head, Mr Beach, known to all as Beachy Head. And he's scarier than Godzilla. Like today, when I gently explained to him why my history essay might be a tiny bit delayed, he immediately clenched his teeth like a ferocious bulldog and snapped, 'I want your essay in my hand first thing Tuesday morning and I very much hope, for your sake, that it's a good one.'

I'm not at all hopeful about it being good. Or even average. But it isn't really my fault, as I try my hardest to listen to his lessons. But there's something about Beachy Head's voice which sends my ears instantly to sleep.

On the bright side, I have managed to write twelve whole lines. On the not so bright side, that's actually my entire essay. Still, they always say, leave people wanting more. And maybe it's better than I think.

7.40 p.m.
No, I don't think so either.

7.41 p.m.
There's something you should know about me and school.

We don't get on.

I've never liked it, never fitted in. But I'm stuck there with teachers in my face all day long. And if you asked any of them about me I know exactly what they'd say: 'Louis is ludicrously dim and extremely lazy.'

But I'm not – well, I'm not lazy anyway, because every single night I study for hours. Only it's a subject we never spend a second on at school – comedy.

And I'm as good at telling jokes, as I am rubbish at all my lessons.

So my dream, my one and only ambition, is to be a comedian. But first I have to be discovered. And for that you need an agent.

Well, I've got one.

Maddy goes to a different school to me. We met at a drama club, as she loves acting. But unfortunately she gets such a massive attack of nerves every time she steps onto a stage, she has had to give up on her dream of being a world-famous actress. And she has decided to become an agent instead.

I'm her very first client, and already she's helped me to appear on a television talent show called *Kids with Attitude*. It's on a satellite channel, so maybe you haven't seen it yet. But trust me, it's awesome.

Each week there are twelve contestants and viewers vote for their winner. They all go on to the Grand Final. The All Winners show. And the winner of that will get their own half-hour Christmas show.

Well, I went on the show – telling jokes. I *so* wanted to win.

I came second. A parrot beat me. The shame of it, I know. I was like totally crushed until they decided one of the runners-up would also be allowed on the winners' show.

And they chose – me.

Any day now they are going to ring up with the date of the All Winners Show and then – well, Maddy is totally convinced I'll win outright this time. That means I'll also get my own Christmas show, and after that I just won't have time to go to school any more. I'll be far too busy travelling the world making people laugh and generally leading the life of an international jet-setter.

8.10 p.m.

One more thing I should have told you about Maddy and me is that she's not only my agent and friend – she's also just become my girlfriend. We haven't actually been out on any dates yet. Well, you've got to build up to that, haven't you?

But I think it's time I got cracking on that.

8.25 p.m.

Just rang Maddy. Right away she said excitedly, '*Kids with Attitude* haven't …?'

'No, not yet, but I called you, Maddy, to find out when you'd like to meet up for our' – I lowered my voice here without quite knowing why – 'first date?'

Immediately she sounded a bit flustered. 'Well, er, when do you think?'

'I've cleared my diary for you,' I said. (Heard someone say that on a TV show once and thought it had sounded pretty cool.) 'So you just name the time and place and I will be there. In person.' I was sounding dead relaxed, but actually I had this odd sort of beating in my heart.

'What about Friday evening?' she suggested.

'It is in my diary already. Would you like to go to Luigi's?'

'Only if we go halves, as it's very expensive.'

'Money is never a problem, Maddy, when I ask a girl out.' How suave was that? And just to make it really clear, I added, 'So I'm paying for you too.'

After I put the phone down, my heart was still beating weirdly fast. This really is it.

Tuesday November 19th

7.25 a.m.

Woken up by Elliot charging into my room, yelling, 'Fire! Fire! Isn't it brilliant?'

'What are you talking about?' I began. Then I heard the smoke alarms doing their stuff downstairs and sprang out of bed.

A bleary-eyed Mum joined us on the landing. 'What's happening, and where's your dad?'

At that moment Dad dashed out of the kitchen.

'Hey, everyone,' he called up to us. 'Sorry for disturbing your sleep. But there's absolutely nothing to worry about.'

'Why have the smoke alarms gone off, then?' asked Elliot.

'Just a tiny little accident. I thought I'd surprise you with warm croissants for breakfast, but I put them in the toaster ...'

'Oh, Dad,' began Elliot.

'It was a lovely thought,' trilled Mum as smoke started billowing up the stairs, 'and no harm done.'

After Dad had sped into the kitchen again, Elliot muttered, 'I hate croissants and—'

'Don't say that,' interrupted Mum. 'This can't be easy for your dad.'

'Not easy for us either,' said Elliot, 'having to eat all his food.' Elliot stomped downstairs again and then called, 'Mum, we've run out of milk.'

'Not your mum's problem!' shouted Dad. 'And I'm on to it,' he added as he tore out of the house.

9.00 a.m.
Beachy Head moves like a panther. I don't mean he walks around on all fours (I'd love to see him doing that), but you don't even realize he's nearby until you feel his hot breath right on

19

your neck.

I'd only arrived at school for a millionth of a second when I got a full blast of hot air. I whirled round. There was Beachy Head, glaring down at me.

'I hope you have your essay with you,' he growled.

I dug about in my bag and brought out my history exercise book. 'It's all in there,' I said, and to lighten the atmosphere I added, 'Enjoy.'

Not a flicker of a smile back. He just glided soundlessly away with my exercise book tucked under his arm.

9.05 a.m.

Do you know what I wish? That we still did colouring-in, at school. I was incredibly good at that. But I guess I peaked too early, as now I'm solidly rubbish at everything. Still, you never have to worry being bottom of the class when I'm around.

3.20 p.m.

It was the last lesson of the day – double maths – when the school secretary bustled in. She thinks she's so important and struts about with a permanent smell under her nose. Anyway, she whispered something to the teacher. I was hoping she was saying the drains had packed up and we all had to go home for a month.

But instead the teacher announced that Beachy Head (only he didn't call him that, of course) wanted to see me immediately. I left to whispers of, 'Oooh, who's in big trouble?'

Beachy Head had obviously read my history essay. (Well, it wouldn't take him very long, would it?) But why couldn't he just have written something rude at the bottom of it like a normal teacher? Why did he have to go to all the bother of seeing me?

The secretary escorted me to Beachy Head's lair, and then walked briskly away. I knocked on his door. I didn't hear anything. But he was pretty ancient and probably a bit deaf, so I knocked again, more loudly, and then I gave several raps all together. He must have heard that.

He did. The door burst open so violently it nearly flew off its hinges. And he stood there, breathing fire at me. 'What on earth do you think you are doing?'

Talk about daft questions, but I explained ever so patiently, 'I'm knocking on your door, as you said you wanted to see me – but I can go away again if you've changed your mind,' I added eagerly. 'And I won't be offended at all.'

'I will tell you when I wish to see you,' said Beachy Head. But he just had, hadn't he? 'For now, you will station yourself outside my room and wait there until I decide to send for you.'

So I'm being told off for going to see him – when he'd just told me to go and see him. I tell you, all adults are completely bonkers.

3.35 p.m.
The school bell has rung. It's the end of school, so by rights I could just go home. This is my time now.

3.45 p.m.
Yeah, I'm still hanging about outside Beachy Head's room. I really, really hate waiting around like this. So to cheer us all up, here's a joke. An educational one, as well.

In ancient times, when a knight was killed in battle, what sign did they put on his grave?
Rust in Peace.

I really love that one. Would you like another one? Sorry, no time, as Beachy Head has just shouted through the door, 'You may come in now.'

Got a horrible feeling I'm not going to enjoy what happens next.

Chapter Three
Poison Pen Letter

4.25 p.m.
And I didn't.

Beachy Head never even said hello to me, or asked if I wanted to sit down, which is not very good manners, is it? He just snapped, 'If I don't answer the door immediately it's for a reason. What could that be?'

'You were having a little nap.'

This wasn't the right answer.

'It's because I am very busy dealing on the phone with someone else.' Now that was perfectly fine with me. But he was acting as if I'd wanted to drop in on him and this was a huge treat for me.

He stood up – a tallish man with heavy glasses, ink-black eyebrows, flowers growing out of his ears and a blotchy, mustard-coloured beard which, as usual, had half his lunch left on it.

'What grade do you think you got for your essay?' And he leaned over me as I struggled to answer.

'Probably not the highest, as it was a bit on the short side. But I know what a busy man you are,' I added desperately. 'So I thought I'd write something brief – but good.'

'Good?' he thundered, causing an old bit of egg to fall out of his beard and onto my hair. 'It was appalling, but of course you're going to be discovered soon, so it doesn't actually matter. And I'm very sorry for taking up so much of your time.'

NO, NOT REALLY. He didn't say any of that last bit. But I so wish he had. Instead, he bored me half to death by going on and on about how I had fallen into the 'rut of laziness and disruptiveness', but he was determined to lift me out of it. The really terrible part, though, was still to come. That was when he handed me a private and confidential letter and said it was for my parents' eyes only.

Of course, the very second I was out of school

I read it. And afterwards I wasn't so much angry as hurt.

Beachy Head made me sound like the world's biggest troublemaker. And that's not me at all. It's just – well, the comedian Joan Rivers said, 'Every time you make someone laugh you give them a little holiday.' And that's all I want to do, give everyone a little holiday from the greyness of school. That's not bad, is it? Thanks so much for agreeing with me.

Anyway, the letter ended by saying Beachy Head wanted to have a discussion about my future with my mum and dad. So would they kindly fix up a time with the office when they could swing by?

Now what should I do?

I straightaway called Maddy.

She immediately asked, 'If your parents see that, will they be so angry they won't allow you to appear on—?'

'Don't even finish that sentence,' I interrupted.

There was silence for a moment as the full horror of what Maddy had nearly said swept over us. For if my parents stopped me going on *Kids with Attitude*, I might not get another chance, which meant I'd remain an undiscovered comedy icon for ever.

'I've decided I won't put my parents to all the

trouble of reading this letter,' I said. 'Well, it will only upset them. So I'm being kind, really.'

'Exceptionally kind,' Maddy agreed.

'But will I get away with it?' I asked.

After only a couple of seconds – her brainpower is truly amazing – Maddy said, 'The reason the school sent a letter was because of its highly confidential nature. So they won't send your parents a text about it, except …'

'Yes.'

'If they don't get a reply, then the school might text your mum and dad asking if they'd seen it.'

'So the school must have a reply dead fast,' I said.

'I'm writing it now,' said Maddy.

Chapter Four

Brain Transplant Urgently Needed

7.00 p.m.

'A light, healthy meal tonight,' announced Dad proudly, before serving up scrambled eggs that bore a very strong resemblance to watery custard.

'You need a spoon to eat this,' cried Elliot.

'That doesn't matter,' said Mum briskly, then in a low voice to Dad, 'You just put in too much milk, that's all – I'm always doing that myself.'

Swimming in the scrambled egg were some burnt mushrooms and chips, while a bowl of rather defeated-looking lettuce was plonked in the middle of the table. For afters, we had some chopped-up bits of manky old fruit.

'How about a take-away tomorrow,' asked Elliot brightly?

8.30 p.m.
Maddy's just called round with my letter for Beachy Head. We decided it was too risky to discuss it in my house. So we went for a little walk.

With something of a flourish she produced the reply.

Here's what it said.

Dear Mr Beach,
Thank you kindly for your recent communication. Its contents have been duly noted and thoroughly digested.

I regret to inform you that I have recently lost my job. I am so depressed about this that I never leave the house now. My wife has got a job but is away all day and is highly exhausted when she comes home. So neither of us will be able to call on you.

I am sure Louis will settle in soon. Rest assured we always talk about world events with him.

Wishing you continued success in your career.

Your humble servant,

Marlon (alias Louis's dad)

After I'd finished reading I let out a slow whistle of approval.

'That letter … it's so genius.'

'I wouldn't go quite that far,' began Maddy modestly.

'No, that bit about Dad not being able to leave the house …'

'You liked that?' She smiled at me eagerly.

'Diabolically clever,' I said. 'Beachy Head will be sobbing into his beard by the time he's finished it. I'll hand that in first thing tomorrow – with pride.' Then I added, 'I've booked up Luigi's for Friday. So that's a definite date.'

'Our very first,' said Maddy softly.

All at once she was looking right at me. I think she was expecting me to say something else – but what? Finally I said, 'Make sure you eat loads and loads. And don't worry about spaghetti dribbling down your chin. Just let it dribble, I say.'

I'm sure that's what she wanted to hear.

Wednesday November 20th

12.40 p.m.
Handed in 'Dad's' letter to Beachy Head's secretary before the start of school. That's

one problem solved, I thought. So I got a truly massive shock when at the end of morning lessons, Beachy Head sent for me.

My class went wild. '*Who's* about to be suspended?' announced one boy gleefully, while another hissed into my ear, 'They say when Beachy Head gets really mad his eyes change colour to black. Tell us if it's true.'

I fronted it out. 'The man just likes my company. So what can I do?' But inside, I was quaking. I mean, I only saw him yesterday. So why is he sending for me again?

1.05 p.m.
This time Beachy Head said, 'Come in' the moment I knocked on the door and actually invited me to sit down in quite a friendly way. Weird, I thought.

It was about to get much weirder.

At first he just sat staring at me, his face all contorted – I thought he might be having a kind of seizure. I sort of hoped he was, actually. Then I could escape out of here. But finally I realized he was trying to smile at me.

He said, 'I've read the ... er ... er interesting letter your father sent to me.'

Just stopped myself from chipping in, 'Yeah, good, wasn't it?'

'Your father informs me he is currently out of work.'

'Oh, he told you that, did he?' I looked surprised, which I thought was a good touch. 'He doesn't tell many people. But yeah, he was in sales and now he's not. It happened very suddenly too.'

'Oh, did it?' Beachy Head leaned forward. 'So it must have been a big shock to him.'

'Massive,' I agreed. Then just for emphasis I added, 'Totally huge.'

'And he also tells me,' Beachy Head lowered his voice, 'he doesn't leave the house very much now.'

'No, he hasn't left for weeks and weeks now. Still, the last time Dad did leave ...' I sighed heavily.

'What happened?' asked Beachy Head, all attention now.

'He popped off to get a tattoo.'

Beachy Head let out a low groan.

'I've never been allowed to see it. They won't even tell me where it is. But Mum was so furious. And Dad hasn't left the house since.'

Beachy Head plucked his beard thoughtfully. He was dead fascinated by all the rubbish I'd just told him.

So I carried on, 'Dad has his good days and his

31

not so good days. Mum says he's going through some stuff right now and we've just got to help him all we can.'

'And I'm sure you do.'

I smiled virtuously. 'I try my best.'

'But you must keep up with your schoolwork.'

'Oh, must I ...? I mean, yes, I must.'

'That's why from now on I'm going to keep a special eye on you.'

This wasn't so good.

'Starting with my subject,' he continued. 'I want you to really try hard with the essay I set your class on *The Changing Economic Conditions during the last years of the reign of Elizabeth I.*'

I'd struggled to stay awake when I was writing down the title.

'Now it's due in on Friday, so I want you to bring it here to me just before the start of school and I will go through it with you, personally.'

'Oh, I don't like to put you to all that bother ...' I began.

I was interrupted by Beachy Head giving a loud, trumpeting sneeze, after which his grey beard was brightened up by tiny glistening globules of snot. 'It's no trouble,' he spluttered through his brown hankie. 'You need helping and encouraging, so I shall do that.'

I started walking towards to the door.

'I will also ring your father.'

I stopped walking. I nearly stopped breathing too.

'Oh, he never answers the phone,' I said quickly. 'He just sits and thinks – and rocks sometimes. Mum says we mustn't bother him when he's rocking or singing. He can sing for hours all by himself.'

'Can he?' said Beachy Head, lost in thought for a moment. Then he contorted his face again. 'Don't worry, Louis; I see how difficult things are for you, but I'm going to help you.'

So now I've got to try and write an essay on something deeply boring which I know nothing about, and then stand there while Beachy Head reads it.

What can I do?

1.10 p.m.
There's only one thing I can do. Get a brain transplant fast!

Chapter Five

A Genius Idea

5.20 p.m.

I hadn't even put my key in the lock when Dad popped up from the back garden.

'I've been hosing down the wheelie bins.'

'It's party time round here, isn't it?'

'It's amazing how dirty they'd got.'

'I'm sure it is,' I said, edging away from him. 'You must tell me all about it, one long winter's night.'

'Elliot starts his rehearsals for *Oliver* tonight,' went on Dad.

'Yeah, he's playing the Artful Dodger. Talk about good casting.'

Dad laughed and said, 'Your mum said she

can pick him up tonight and every night he's rehearsing.'

I knew Elliot would be pleased about that. He'd told me that when Dad was waiting for him after school, he stood there right in the middle of all the mums, looking so fantastically awkward and embarrassed that Elliot wanted to walk right past him.

I quickly peered about. No, Dad hadn't left me a snack anywhere, as Mum would have done. He really was a rubbish stay-at-home Dad. I was, of course, far too exhausted to prepare anything myself.

Then Dad announced, 'I thought you and I could spend some quality time tonight.'

I looked at him in frozen horror. Surely Dad knew there were a thousand things I should be doing now, and not one of them involved talking to him.

'I've been looking forward to it, actually,' Dad went on eagerly. 'You and I, hanging out.' Such enthusiasm for my company is extremely rare, so I thought, All right, I could spare Dad five minutes – and I hadn't even checked Facebook yet – out of my extremely crowded just-home-from-school schedule. But five minutes turned into twenty, which became practically a whole precious hour.

Now I did realize Dad had been on his own all day. But honestly, Robinson Crusoe just after he'd been rescued couldn't have been chattier. And then Dad asked, 'How would you like to surprise your Mum?'

'Jump out at her when she comes in, you mean?'

'No,' said Dad. 'What about if we give the dining room table a really good scrub?'

He'd said, 'WE.' And I'd only just got home from school as well. This was nothing less than child labour. No wonder I could only gape at him at first.

'Or we could just surprise Mum with a good knock, knock joke,' I suggested desperately.

But it was too late. Dad was already filling a bowl with soapy water and handing me a sponge.

Most amazing was how excited Dad looked when he was doing something so sensationally boring. Sometimes I think my parents will always remain a mystery to me.

'Let's really get stuck in,' said Dad, 'as your mum will be home any minute.'

And we were both still scrubbing away when we heard – well I suppose you'd call it a yelp really. Then Mum yipped, 'But you're taking off all the polish when you clean it like that ... just stop!'

We stopped and I murmured to Dad. 'Might have been better if we'd just surprised Mum with a knock, knock joke.'

5.43 p.m.
Mum's been getting all excited about the kitchen floor. Dad must have cleaned it today or something. And she was saying to me, 'Your dad's done such a wonderful job, hasn't he?' I think she was trying to make up for being so mad at him earlier.

Then Dad said to her, 'I'm really enjoying doing all these mindless tasks. It is very calming and it's helping me to recharge my batteries.' Mum gave him such an odd look then.

7.10 p.m.
Maddy's just sent me acres of notes about Elizabeth I. So how hard can it be to write an essay about her?

7.25 p.m.
Dead hard.

7.45 p.m.
My excuse for Beachy Head as to why I can't hand in my history essay:

Some aliens from outer space (they didn't

specify which planet they were from and I didn't like to press them) have borrowed my essay so they can study how the human brain works. They didn't say when they'd be returning it either. But it might be quite a while.

7.52 p.m.
I really like that excuse – so original for a start. But will Beachy Head believe it?

7.53 p.m.
Not a hope.

7.55 p.m.
Anyway, I can't think about that any more as I've still got all my comedy homework to do. Any second now *Kids with Attitude* will call. And I've got to make sure I'm ready. So every night I'm adding more jokes to my joke collection, then studying a DVD – currently season three of *Modern Family* – and I always fall asleep laughing at a funny book. Right now it's another Jeeves and Wooster story, *The Mating Season* by P.G. Wodehouse.

I'd totally recommend this homework, as the world of comedy is a magical place to escape to. It's also how real life should be.

Thursday November 21st

5.40 p.m.
Just had a genius idea.

First of all, you should know Mum has very strict views about homework. She's always spouting this guff about how I'm not learning anything if she does it. So she has never done a single sum for me, or written even one sentence. Talk about child neglect. But Mum wasn't here when I got home, polluting the atmosphere with her views.

That's why I had the idea of very casually asking Dad if he knew anything about Elizabeth I, as I didn't, and I had to hand my essay in personally to Beachy Head tomorrow, who really had it in for me. I gulped a bit there too.

Dad looked at me. 'I was pretty good at history actually – even got a prize for it once.'

'Hey, Dad, I never knew that.'

'But I don't think I can write your history essay for you.'

I acted shocked at the very idea. 'Of course not, and I'd never ask you to do that, even though there is an ancient law, as old as time itself, that if you can't do your homework you ask your parents to do it. How about just getting me started?' I threw in an extra little gulp here.

But I needn't have bothered with that gulp as Dad was already staring hard at the question, keen to see if he could re-awaken his old history magic.

I handed him all the stuff Maddy had run off for me from the Internet. Dad studied it very carefully and then started writing at the kitchen table. But a few minutes later he tore it up. 'Not good enough,' he muttered.

'You'll get there, Dad – I've total confidence in you,' I said encouragingly.

Dad was really intent now. This time when he started writing he didn't stop, his pen just flew across the page. And when finally he finished he said apologetically, 'I'm afraid I've written the whole essay for you.'

'Never mind,' I said. 'I like your enthusiasm.'

I started reading. I didn't understand a word of it, so I knew it must be good. 'This is ace, Dad,'

'I'm a bit rusty.'

'No, this is awesome stuff.'

'Well, do you know what?' said Dad. 'I really enjoyed getting stuck into a history essay again.'

And I'd really enjoyed watching him do my homework too.

So everyone was hideously happy really.

I suppose when you think about it, Dad has until recently led the easy carefree life of someone who just went to work every day. But now he's stuck at home serving up food that no one can eat, and that must knock his confidence a bit.

Doing my history essay has really put a spring back in his step again. I'm just so glad I was able to help him out.

6.45 p.m.
I think I shall be helping Dad out much more in the future too.

Chapter Six

Remembering Not to Pick My Nose

Friday November 22nd

9.30 a.m.
I was actually looking forward to handing in my history essay to Beachy Head – even felt a bit of a swot. OK, Dad had written it, but I'd had to copy it all out. And that took time. So it was a joint effort really, wasn't it?

But Beachy Head was suddenly far too busy to see me. And I could only deliver it to his secretary. I'd so love to see Beachy Head's face when he is reading it. He is going to be totally amazed by my academic brilliance.

5.00 p.m.
So here it is. Nearly.

My first date with Maddy.

It's a big deal and yet sort of isn't. I mean, I've never been out with a girl before. Not on an official date. But it isn't as if I'm dating a total stranger. Actually I know Maddy better than anyone, so I shouldn't be nervous.

5.02 p.m.
And I so am.

5.52 p.m.
I'm only wearing my normal clothes tonight. I know Maddy wouldn't want me to make any special fuss. I'll hurl on masses of deodorant, though, as sometimes I smell a bit. That isn't because I don't wash – I had a shower two weeks ago. No, it's because of all my teenage hormones surging about. They're stinky, not me.

Anyway, I must have overdone the deodorant as Elliot dived into my room coughing wildly and yelling, 'Phew, you totally pong, keep your bedroom door closed or we'll all pass out.'

Then Mum appeared and sniffed a bit before looking at me questioningly. She gave a little smile. 'You're seeing Maddy tonight.'

'Correct, score five points.'

'But tonight wouldn't be …?' She gave a coy little laugh. 'It wouldn't be a *date*, would it?'

'I believe that is the correct technical term, yes, Mum.'

'Why didn't you didn't tell us?' she cooed. 'You and Maddy … aaah.'

'Mum, we're not puppies.'

'And where are you taking Maddy?'

'Er … Luigi's.' For some annoying reason I was also blushing furiously.

'How lovely. This is a big moment in your—'

'I think we're done here Mum,' I interrupted.

So she went off and I thought, Great, that's all over with, because the very last thing I wanted was a fuss. But then I was summoned downstairs. They were both waiting for me.

'Come and sit down,' said Dad.

'Really,' I murmured.

'We're both so pleased that you are taking Maddy to Luigi's for your first proper date. We can remember what a big moment that is.' Mum stopped here to smirk at Dad. 'And we wondered if you had any questions at all?'

'About Luigi's?' I asked.

'No,' said Mum a bit impatiently. 'About …' She hesitated. 'Relationships.'

Dad chipped in, 'Ask us anything, as I can still remember what it's like taking a really hot girl out.'

I immediately put my hands over my ears. 'Oh, gross. No more details please.'

'That really hot girl,' said Dad, 'was, of course, your mother.'

'Still gross,' I said firmly. 'But I'll leave you to enjoy your golden memories as I haven't any questions. So thanks for this – it's been really average.' I stood up.

'Sit down, we haven't finished, Louis,' said Mum. 'We've some little tips for you.'

'There's no need and I'm sure you have better things to do, I know I have,' I added under my breath. But it was hopeless. They were off.

'We're just going to point out to you a little habit of yours,' went on Mum, 'which you might want to think about.'

'What little habit?' I demanded.

'Well, whenever we went out for a meal as a family you always used to rather absent-mindedly pick your nose,' said Mum.

'When I was about two weeks old ...'

'We haven't noticed you doing it recently,' admitted Mum, 'but watch out for that. And' – she gave a tinkling laugh – 'do put a comb through your hair and remember to iron the shirt you're wearing.'

'Mum, I'm not going for a job interview.'

'And polish your shoes,' she went on.

'I'll be wearing trainers actually, because I'm not going out for a meal in the Victorian age.'

'You still need to make sure they're clean,' said Mum. 'Whenever I meet a young man the first thing I do is check his shoes.'

'Mum, that's just weird.'

'And one other little tip,' said Dad. 'There's no need to shout.'

'I don't shout!' I shouted.

'You've got one of those voices which carries,' said Mum. 'So try and talk more quietly. Practise in your bedroom.'

'It's far more romantic,' said Dad.

'And another thing ...' went on Mum.

I closed my eyes. Was this never going to end? They were driving me crazy.

'Tonight, don't talk about yourself. Ask Maddy some questions.'

'Like, what's her name?'

'Ask Maddy questions about herself,' said Mum.

'But I know all about her.'

Mum gave a little smile. 'I'm sure there are some things you don't know, Louis. Try and think what they are.'

Then Dad smiled at me. 'Hope we've helped you tonight.'

Oh sure, Dad, I was nervous before. Now I'm a total wreck.

6.05 p.m.

Who is the very last person I'd want to see before going on a date with Maddy?

Her ex, that's who.

Yes, Maddy had a boyfriend before me. For about four minutes.

Edgar.

Edgar is also Maddy's only other client. He doesn't go to school and is taught at home because he finds people his own age 'hopelessly immature'. His main hobby is writing terrible poems. I felt sorry for Maddy having to spend time with him – until she announced he was her boyfriend.

I was totally shocked and horrified. But as I mentioned, they didn't go out together for very long. Edgar dumped her actually – but only because he knew there was only one boy Maddy was really interested in – me.

But now here he was again, on my doorstep, his black hair even curlier than I'd remembered. He is the one boy incidentally who doesn't smell, ever. Soap seems to ooze off him.

'Maddy was kind enough to inform me,' he began (he always speaks as if he's ninety-six-years old) 'of your engagement at Luigi's tonight. She told me, because I had invited her to my house to celebrate my thirteenth birthday today.'

'Happy birthday,' I said. 'You don't look a day over twelve.'

'So will you please pass on my regards to Maddy?'

'I'll put that on my list of things not to do,' I replied.

'And I have some advice for you. Maddy enjoys good, intelligent conversation. So you will certainly need to prepare for that.'

'I know all about Maddy,' I said quietly.

'I hope you do,' he replied. 'Now may I ask you a question?'

'I love questions.'

'Do you ever think about the person you wish you were?' Before I could reply he went on, 'Well, right now I wish I were you. Something I never ever thought would happen.'

Chapter Seven

A Date with the Elephant Woman

6.24 p.m.

Dad was driving me to Luigi's. And Mum waved me off as if I were leaving for the Foreign Legion. 'Do give Maddy our love,' she said. 'And we want to hear all about it tonight.'

'I don't,' said Elliot.

'It'll probably be on the ten o'clock news,' I said.

Then Mum called after me, 'Louis, have you got a handkerchief?'

I turned round, 'No, I thought I'd just wipe my nose on my sleeve.' Then Mum looked so alarmed I had to add hastily, 'That's a joke, Mum. Actually I've got two – just in case Maddy wants a clean one.'

As I got into the car Elliot started yelling for some obscure reason, 'Kiss my feet, they smell so sweet.'

All my family are mad.

6.45 p.m.

I'm in Luigi's sitting at a table with two chairs – yeah, no expense spared tonight. It's a posh place – leather seats and dark woodwork – and packed already, mainly with couples a bit older than Maddy and me. Maddy isn't here yet, but the table was booked for seven o'clock so she's not late at all – I'm just a bit early. Meanwhile, outside it's started to rain, in case you're at all interested, which I'm sure you're not, but I don't know what else to write.

I really hate waiting for dates to start.

6.50 p.m.

Been telling myself I've just got to relax and be cool. That's the most important thing on dates, isn't it? – to act super-cool at all times.

I've also been imagining Maddy and me kissing. I mean, we've had a few little kisses before, but they weren't very different from the ones I doled out to my aunties at Christmas. Tonight I want to sweep Maddy off her feet. And if at the end of our kiss tonight she whispers, 'Wow, Louis,' or just 'Wow' in fact, I'll be so happy and proud.

6.54 p.m.
To get warmed up, I've had a quick practice by kissing my hand. I want to make sure I get the right speed and pressure.

6.56 p.m.
Just realized the girl on the next table has been watching me kiss my hand. I immediately stopped and tried smiling at her. Then she just looked scared. So now I've stopped smiling and kissing my hand.

7.02 p.m.
Maddy is two minutes late. Not that it matters. That's why I'm going to write about something else. Like, well, the rain is really thrashing down now. And all the customers are coming in shaking themselves exactly the way dogs do.

Anything else to tell you? Yeah, there are warm food smells all around me. I'm sure I'll be really hungry when Maddy turns up, which will be any second now.

7.05 p.m.
Maddy's five minutes late. Is that ever so slightly ominous? She is normally very punctual.

7.10 p.m.
She's now ten minutes late. Shall I text her, just to check everything is all right?

7.11 p.m.
Far too desperate. And I've got to act cool at all times! Why do I keep forgetting that?

7.15 p.m.
I'm sure I caught the waiter giving me the pity look. He thinks I've been stood up.

7.16 p.m.
That girl on the other table is also looking at me again. I can imagine her talking about me later: *There was this really weird boy on the next table to me, just sat there all on his own, kissing his hand!*

7.20 p.m.
Maddy is now exactly twenty minutes late. What on earth's happened? Should I send her a very laid-back text? Just to make certain she is still coming. Well, I could do that normally, but not

when I'm on a date. The rules are all changed.

7.28 p.m.
Panic over. I've just spotted Maddy, which would be great except – well, she arrived with her two older sisters, one either side of her like bodyguards. And I suppose there's nothing wrong with that, except all three of them are whispering away, and it looks to me as if they're both trying to persuade Maddy not to make a run for it.

No, I'm being stupid, except – well, Maddy does look incredibly miserable. You'd think she was about to sit a five-hour exam rather than spend time with a handsome, hilarious guy. (That's me, in case you're wondering.)

And what could she be whispering to her sisters about? What's so important?

Now, at last, the sisters are leaving. This date is FINALLY about to start.

8.00 p.m.
When Maddy arrived at my table she stopped looking gloomy. In fact, she was smiling. 'I'm sorry I'm so late, Louis.'

'Are you? I didn't even notice,' I said, which I thought sounded pretty cool and relaxed. And I slouched back in my leather seat to emphasize how laid-back I was.

She sat down opposite me. And I waited for Maddy to take her coat off. But she didn't. In fact, she even kept her hood up. This seemed to suggest she wasn't planning to stay very long.

'Are you OK?' I asked.

'Yes, why?' She immediately sounded suspicious, jumpy.

'Oh, no reason, I just wondered why ...' My voice fell away. Best not to ask why she was keeping her coat on. Maybe it was something girls did when they were on first dates. I wish I'd done more research now.

And then for the first time ever Maddy and I ran out of conversation. Normally we can gabble away for hours. But tonight we were like two strangers meeting for the first time.

'Ha ha,' I said at last, thinking you can't go wrong with 'Ha ha.' So I said it again. But you can't go on saying 'ha ha' for too long either. So, remembering my parents' advice to lower my voice, I said, 'Maddy, here we are then, on our first ever date.'

'Say that again,' she said.

'Here we are on our first ever date.'

'I'm sorry.' She leaned forward.

'I just said here we are on our first ever date.'

Maddy nodded, rather gloomily I thought,

and still with her hood up too.

Then giving what I hoped was a James Bond smile I whispered, 'Shall we check out the menu together?'

'Say again,' said Maddy, leaning even further forward.

I tried again, letting another James Bond grin play across my face. 'Shall we check out the menu together?'

Maddy stood up and actually leaned over me, 'I'm sorry, but suddenly I can't hear a word you say.'

I thrust a menu at her. 'Do you want some food?' I asked in my normal voice.

'Actually, I'm not very hungry,' said Maddy, sitting down again.

Oddly enough, I wasn't either. And I spend most of my life feeling starving. In fact, just about every minute of it – except now.

'How about if we skip the starters?' she asked.

'Well, if you want to.'

I was a bit hurt. I had a horrible feeling Maddy would have liked to skip the main course too. But eventually she found something on the menu she liked – a jacket potato with cheese.

'Is that all?' I asked. 'Would you …?'

'No, a jacket potato would be just perfect.'

'Provided my dad's not cooking it.' I'd told

Maddy all about my dad's culinary disasters, and we did have a bit of a laugh about that.

Then the waiter materialized. He frowned very sadly when Maddy gave her order. 'You ordered that off our lunch-time menu, didn't you?' He shook his head gravely. 'No baked potatoes are available after three o'clock.'

'But why not?' I demanded. 'It's not against the law to eat a baked potato at night. Well, if it is, it's the first I've heard of it.'

'No, no, it's all right, honestly,' said Maddy, her face a deep red now. She ended up ordering the same as me – steak and chips.

After the waiter had gone I said, 'What an idiot! You can't have baked potatoes after three o'clock, like there's some weird curfew or something. I'm dead sorry, Maddy.'

'It's not your fault.' She smiled.

And for a moment we both started to relax. Then she leaned back and actually took her coat and hood off. That had to be a good sign. I glanced at her hair.

It was different to how it usually is. It had gone all curly and frizzy, or rather parts of it had – some of the curls seemed to have fallen out already. It probably wasn't a great look for her, to be honest. But it made an interesting change.

I was about to say this when she cried, 'Yes, I know, Louis.'

'Ha ha,' I replied. Not quite sure what she knew and assumed I knew too.

'I know, I look exactly like the Elephant Man,' she cried.

'Ha ha,' I said yet again. 'Surely you mean the Elephant *Woman*.' Insane as it seems now, I was trying to make a tiny little joke.

But Maddy just went berserk. 'Did you just say I look like the Elephant Woman?'

'No, you said that.'

'I didn't.' Her voice rose. 'I said I looked like the Elephant Man. Then you said yes, you look minging.'

'Maddy, what are you talking about? I never said you looked minging. I just said you looked like the Elephant Woman.' For some reason I shouted those last words right across the restaurant. And that wasn't what I'd meant to say at all. But now it was as if my brain had turned to mush.

Maddy looked as if she was about to burst into tears.

Desperate now, I said, 'Look, I'd never say to anyone they looked minging, even if they did. And you so don't.'

'I know I do,' mumbled Maddy,

57

'What are you talking about – your hair looks great, actually.'

'It really doesn't.'

'No, it does, honestly.'

'Yeah, I like fun hair.'

Immediately Maddy looked upset again. 'Are you saying I look funny?'

'No, no, will you just listen to me.' I was getting really stressed now, something I hardly ever do. 'When I said it was fun hair, I meant it was hair that makes you feel good and cheers you up.'

Desperate now to talk about something – anything else – I remembered Mum's advice to pay Maddy a compliment. 'And your dress is great, sensational. I mean, I can't tell you how much I like it. I really, really like it. Not that I want to borrow it or anything,' I laughed wildly.

'You have seen this dress before,' said Maddy. 'Don't you remember?'

I could hardly even remember my name at the moment.

Then Maddy got up.

'You're not leaving?' I was only half joking.

'No, just going to the loo, if that's all right with you.'

'Yes, carry on, and they've got very impressive loos here – not that I've ever been in the Ladies,

58

of course, but I peeped through the window once – only joking.' What in the name of sanity was I talking about? I hadn't a clue.

Anyway, Maddy left after that. And she's still not back. You don't think she's scarpered off home, do you, leaving me to eat two plates of steak and chips?

8.13 p.m.
She's coming back. That's a relief. She must have been fiddling with her hair, though, as it looks different. I won't even mention that. I'll just brighten things up. That's the one thing I am good at.

8.30 p.m.
Neither Maddy nor me ate much of our steak and chips. And all the time she was there I kept missing Maddy. She was right opposite me but something was different. Something had gone.

But I was a boy on a mission – cheering Maddy up. So I asked her, 'Why were the elephants thrown out of the swimming pool?' She shook her head. *Because they wouldn't keep their trunks on.* Got another one for you, Maddy. Which famous painter always has a cold? *Van Cough*, get it?'

I went on rattling off joke after joke.

I so wanted to make her laugh. I usually can, you know. And she's got a great laugh – surprisingly loud too. But I never heard it tonight, even though I tried my very hardest. So I settled for her smiling. That was something.

And after our truly catastrophic start, at least this date can't get any worse.

9.40 p.m.
You know, I thought this date couldn't get any worse. Ha ha – that's me laughing bitterly.

Ha ha – and that's me doing it again, even more bitterly.

We'd ordered coffees and I was on my way back from the loo when I spotted Maddy wasn't on her own.

Edgar was there with her.

Now, remember when I'd told all my hilarious jokes and Maddy had only smiled politely. Well now, would you believe, she was rocking with laughter – at Edgar!

How dare Maddy laugh more with another boy than me? And when we were on a date as well. That's so insulting, isn't it?

No wonder I marched back to our table with this massive frown on my face. I don't think I even said a proper hello to Edgar. He didn't hang about for very long anyway.

But Maddy didn't seem at all surprised at him suddenly popping up. She muttered something about him liking the milkshakes at the little café next door.

'And he just happened to want a milkshake, the very night …?'

'He only dropped by to say hello. It *is* his birthday.'

The more she defended him, the madder I felt. 'Well, you two seemed to be having a great time.'

'Oh, he does make me laugh,' said Maddy.

'I noticed,' I snarled.

'He said if ever he took a girl out he thinks he'd just invite her round his house to do a jigsaw.' She started to laugh again. 'And then they could have a game of chess—'

'I've just remembered, I don't care *what* he said,' I interrupted.

We were both super silent after that, drinking or rather gulping down our coffees, desperate for it all to be over. I never even tried to kiss her because – well, enough things had gone wrong tonight.

Then when I got home it was as if I were on a contestant or a quiz show, with Mum and Dad firing all these questions at me about tonight, while keeping these soppy little smiles on their faces. But why were they so interested? It would totally creep me out to hear about any of their dates.

Anyway, I fooled them all right by describing a quite different evening. But it wasn't easy. And that's all I can bear to tell you about tonight.

Chapter Eight
Taking a Break

Saturday November 23rd

10.15 a.m.
Woken up by a really disgusting smell. Then
Elliot leaped into my bedroom clutching a
handkerchief to his mouth. 'Either Dad is
cooking breakfast,' he gasped, 'or someone has
just done the smelliest fart ever.'

Downstairs Dad grinned at us through a cloud
of stinkiness. 'It's the full hotel breakfast this
morning – orange juice, tea and toast, porridge
and kippers. Call your mum, will you?'

But there was no need. The smell had called
her.

'This is so amazing, isn't it, boys?' she spluttered.

'That's one word for it,' I muttered.

Somehow Mum kept an expression of joy on her face even when she was eating Dad's brown, lumpy porridge. I never realized she was such a good actress.

2.20 p.m.
Decided to ring Maddy.

We'll have a real laugh about last night now. Maddy can always see the funny side of stuff. That's one of the really great things about her.

2.25 p.m.
Decided not to ring Maddy.

Once you go out with a girl you can't just ring her up when you feel like it, in case it looks needy and desperate. How could I have forgotten that?

So I shall behave like a proper boyfriend, which means waiting for Maddy to ring me.

7.15 p.m.
Maddy always texts me on Saturday. Always. Only not today. OK, it was an awful date, but she could at least have thanked me for paying for everything. It wouldn't have killed her to do that, would it?

10.30 p.m.
Still nothing from Maddy. Next time she pays for herself.

Sunday November 24th

9.15 a.m.
Elliot woke me up yelling excitedly, 'Put away your stomach pump, Mum's cooking breakfast today.'

We tore downstairs, our stomachs turning somersaults of joy. When Dad wandered into the kitchen Mum said quickly, 'You've coped with the cooking all week. It's my turn today.'

I'm absolutely certain I saw a look of relief rush across Dad's face.

5.30 p.m.
At last, a text from Maddy. But she never mentioned our date. She just asked if I'd heard from *Kids with Attitude*. I mean, it's not very likely they'd call me on Sunday, is it? Plus, if they had she'd have been the very first person I'd have told.

That was only an excuse, wasn't it? She wants me to call her.

* * *

65

5.35 p.m.

Maddy told me once I've got one of those faces that instantly cheers you up. That's why I've decided I shan't ring her. I'll go round her house instead.

I'll also say something hilarious about our first date, and then speedily fix up another much-improved one.

6.35 p.m.

Her mum answered the door. Normally she is smiley and chatty. Today she gave me such a sharp look and then said very curtly how Maddy was busy doing her homework so she couldn't talk for long. Left me waiting in the hallway for ages too.

I tell you, the tension was just awful. And I hadn't even seen Maddy yet. I had to do something to lighten the atmosphere, but what? Then I knew. I'd pretend to be an orang-utan. (Some might say I don't have to do much pretending.) That never fails to raise a smile.

So when Maddy finally appeared I immediately let out this orang-utan cry – dead realistic too. You'd really think a fierce but kindly orang-utan had come to call.

I even beat my chest with my fists and then waited for Maddy to fall about laughing. Instead,

66

she glared at me. Then her mum appeared again.

'What on earth was all that noise?' she demanded.

'Just Louis doing his impression of an elephant,' said Maddy.

Maddy's mum gave me a really withering glare before stomping off, while I said, quite insulted, 'Maddy, that was the cry of an orang-utan.'

'Oh, I thought it was an elephant,' she said. 'It sounded just like one.'

'But I was drumming my chest.'

'Oh, were you, I didn't notice. I told my mum how you thought I looked like the Elephant Woman.'

'Actually, I never said that.'

'Yes, you did.'

'Well, I did, but only as a joke because you said—' I stopped. There really was no point in explaining now.

'Anyway, I've changed my hair back,' she announced.

'Great.' The word was out of my mouth before I realized.

'I thought you'd be pleased,' she snapped.

'No, I don't mean great – I mean—' I looked at her desperately. 'Hey, Maddy, you and I have just won an award for the worst first date ever.'

Then I started laughing wildly. Unfortunately I was the only one.

Maddy just looked incredibly hurt suddenly. That was the very last thing I wanted to do. But going out with someone changes everything. Suddenly every conversation is like a minefield. And right now I couldn't say or do anything right. I had to move things forward somehow.

So finally I asked as jauntily as I could, 'Look, Maddy, our next date can only be better. So when would you like to go out with me again?' Then I grinned broadly.

That's when Maddy actually looked away from me. There was a horrible silence too.

'Well, that sounds like a maybe? How about next ...?'

'Actually,' Maddy faced me again, 'I think we should take a break from each other.'

'A break! But we've only had one date.' Then I added in a low whisper, 'You're not ...?' But I didn't even dare finish the sentence because, 'You're dumped' are the two most terrible words you can ever hear from a girl. Especially if you really like her, as I do Maddy.

'Louis, I'm sorry,' she said, 'it's not you, it's me.'

'But you are ...' I whispered hoarsely, 'dumping me?'

'Yes.' Her voice was incredibly whispery too.

'If we could just go back to how we were before, I'd be so happy.'

'Well, I really like to make people happy,' I somehow managed to croak out. 'So I'll ...' But I couldn't say any more – I was too choked up. Instead, I just walked very quickly away. I thought Maddy might call after me to stop as she'd changed her mind and it had all been a terrible misunderstanding. But the only sound I heard was her door slamming shut.

9.30 p.m.
Guess what, I've just written a poem. My first ever. Here's how it starts:

It's grey and damp outside.
But it's even greyer and damper inside my head.

That's also how it ends. I got stuck after that. No doubt Edgar could have written tons more.

Still, I bet if you asked Edgar what a zombie's favourite cereal is he wouldn't know it was Rice Creepies.

Nor would he be able to tell you why the broom was late.

It over-swept.

But I can't send Maddy jokes any more, can I? Not after I've been dumped.

Chapter Nine

A Truly Terrifying Moment

Monday November 25th

12.00 p.m.
Usually I get Z– for my history essays. Today I gained a C. I was practically a swot.

At the end of the lesson Beachy Head said to me. 'A lot of hard work went into this essay, didn't it?'

I could agree with him totally truthfully on that point.

'You just need to explain your conclusion in more detail and give more examples.'

I nodded gravely.

'But you must keep up this standard.'

'Oh, he will—' I hastily corrected myself. 'I mean, I will.'

4.45 p.m.

When I told Dad my history result his face actually fell.

'Hey, don't you dare be disappointed,' I said. 'Me getting a C is earth-shattering. I'm surprised bells didn't ring out everywhere and—'

'Did your teacher say why we didn't get a higher grade?' Dad interrupted.

'He droned on about explaining the conclusion in more detail. And, oh yeah, he said he wanted extra examples. There's no pleasing some people, is there?'

'I suppose no one got an A?' asked Dad.

'From Beachy Head, no way.'

'What about a B?'

'A few,' I said.

'How many?'

I hadn't a clue. 'About ten,' I guessed.

'Ten!' Now Dad looked positively miserable.

'Well, maybe nine or eight or seven ... anyway, there's another history essay this Friday about Elizabeth I's reputation in the last years of her reign.' Dad was on to it before I'd finished speaking.

'I'll get you a B this time,' he promised.

'Now I don't want you exhausting yourself – but a B would be awesome.' Then I added, 'Best if we keep this between ourselves.' As I just knew Mum would twist Dad doing all my history homework into something ugly.

Dad didn't say anything, but I'm certain he nodded his head, very slightly in agreement.

Tuesday November 26th

5.20 p.m.
I'd just got in when Dad rushed over to me. 'I don't want to sound too bragging but I've done all the washing today.'

'I'm thrilled for you,' I murmured.

'It's just a question of organisation really. Give me a hand putting it into the tumble dryer, will you?'

I was stunned. Didn't Dad realize I hadn't been near a computer game all day? But then I pulled out Dad's white shirt and things got a lot more interesting.

For this one was now generously decorated with blobs of blue.

I showed it to Dad. His eyes widened considerably. Then he started frantically pulling

72

out more washing. Much of this – including Mum's blouse and light grey trousers – now had an additional new blue design.

As for the expression on Dad's face – you know in spooky films when the monster first appears and people start reacting. Well I can tell you, they seemed relaxed compared to how horrified Dad looked then.

'But how ... how?' he asked in a tortured sort of voice.

'Did you check everyone's pockets Dad?'

'I didn't check anyone's pockets ... I just piled it all in.'

I shook my head gravely. 'First rule of washing is, you must peek in every single pocket. Even I know that.'

Then Dad pulled out a now mangled, blue pen. It was one of mine too. But I kept quiet about that.

'Now what can I do?' asked Dad, as if I were a leading expert on laundry.

'Hide,' I suggested.

But I could see Dad was in a spot. So I patted his shoulder in a kindly way and said. 'Mum won't be too mad. Well she'll froth a bit at first. But she knows you're just an amateur.'

And then we heard the front door opening.

Mum and Elliot were home.

Mum was laughing about something or other. She sounded in an alarmingly good mood.

'Hi there,' she began as she bounced into the kitchen. 'Oh you have been so busy again ...' but her voice fell away as she spied the results of Dad's hard work. And for a few seconds a thick, dark silence filled the room.

Then Mum held up some of the new two-tone washing.

'In some cases I'd say Dad's improved them,' I said hopefully. 'He's made your blouse a lot more interesting, for a start. So Mum no worries about not being noticed. You'll be the centre of attention wherever you go now...' I stopped. Mum was sighing loudly.

Then she saw Dad's stricken face, swallowed hard and said quietly. 'Accidents will happen.'

6.25 p.m.
On the bright side, Dad's finished my history essay already. He's just handed it to me. 'Talk about keen,' I said. 'It hasn't got to be in until Friday. And after skimming it I declared, 'Dad, this is sheer class.'

'It was a challenge but I enjoyed it.' Then he added, 'I'd better get a B this time.' He was only half joking.

Wednesday November 27th

Just helped Dad put the shopping away. I know I'm too kind hearted. But he was sitting staring at it, all piled up on the kitchen table when I got in. Afterwards he did make me a cup of tea and scattered a few biscuits about.

Then, right out of the blue he said, 'Your date with Maddy didn't go so well on Friday, did it?'

I never saw that coming. Took me completely by surprise. Perhaps that's why I blurted out, 'After only one date Maddy said we should take a break from each other. Mind you, it was a total disaster.'

'Why, what happened?'

I told him every squirm-inducing detail. He just nodded and smiled faintly, which makes you say more, doesn't it? And finally I said, 'But I'm amazed you noticed anything was wrong. I thought I'd put up a pretty good front.'

'You did,' said Dad, 'but I've had so many terrible dates myself, I know all the signs.' And then he didn't start talking about himself and his ancient memories, as most adults would have done. Instead, he apologized.

'Your mum and I didn't help that night, did we?'

'Well ...'

'We got a bit carried away remembering our own first date and bombarding you with tips. Sorry about that.'

'That's OK, just don't do it again.' I was pretty stunned by the way he was talking to me.

Then he said, sounding more like a cool older brother than my dad, 'Give Maddy a bit of space now. Let her come back to you.'

'Not very likely, if she's dumped me after one date,' I said.

'Wait and see,' said Dad. 'But I think she will, and when she does, let her talk. And really listen to what she's saying.' Then he asked, 'Have you heard from her since you broke up?'

'No.'

'Well, I think you should contact her. You are still friends, aren't you?'

'I'm not sure what we are right now.'

'Send her a text.'

'Saying what?' I demanded.

'Anything, say "my dad says hi and asks how you are", if you like. It doesn't matter, but just text her.'

I was dead grateful to Dad, but I also felt embarrassed that I'd blabbed so much highly confidential stuff to him. So I said as a kind of joke, 'What I've told you is a secret you can never tell anyone ever. It's certainly not for Elliot's ears – or Mum's, actually.'

I thought he'd argue with that. But he just patted me on the arm and said, 'It's probably best if you tell your mum when you're ready.'

I bet he does tell her, though.

7.50 p.m.
Just texted Maddy:

Dad says 2 say hi. And how ru.

Then I added. 'What did the stamp say to the envelope? Stick with me and you'll go places.'

Maddy immediately sent a text back, saying hi back to my dad and to tell him she was very well – and she liked the joke. So then I sent her a few more jokes and she liked all of them too.

Thursday November 28th

5.00 p.m.
School was so boring today I nearly forgot to breathe, but just as I'd got home my mobile rang.

It was Evie from *Kids with Attitude*.

We talked for a bit – well, she asked me if I was looking forward to Christmas – then she told me the date of the *Kids with Attitude* Final.

It's Friday December 13th

'For the Final,' said Evie, 'we want you to be your hilarious self, of course, but we also want you to do something unexpected in your act – something a bit different.'

'Like what?' I asked at once.

'That's up to you,' said Evie. 'Maybe you could display another talent.'

'While I'm telling jokes?'

'Yes, that's a good idea,' said Evie. 'But think about it for a bit. We're giving the same instructions to all our contestants, and we can't wait to see what original ideas you come up with. Good luck, Louis.'

6.05 p.m.
Texted Maddy the good news.

She texted back immediately.

She wants me to have my act ready to show her on Saturday. She's also going to try and think of something a bit different to make my performance special. We're getting on so much better, now we've stopped going out together.

7.20 p.m.
Heard Mum and Dad whispering in the kitchen. She was asking, 'Have you been in the boys' bedrooms lately?'

'No, I haven't,' said Dad, 'because of a little idea of mine where we let the boys take total control of their own space.'

'Oh yes,' said Mum very doubtfully.

'I even gave them their own dusters and they seemed really fired up about it.'

'Well, I've just had a little peek and both bedrooms are getting a little bit out of control.' (That's Mum's code for a total mess)

'Well, that does surprise me ... I was sure my new scheme ...' stuttered Dad, and then he stopped.

He sounded so bitterly disappointed that I burst into the kitchen yelling, 'Hey, everyone, I'm just off to do some mad dusting. Can't wait to get stuck in. It's so brilliant having my own private, personal duster.' And upstairs I searched long and hard for that duster. Never found it. But I used my hankie, which is just as good, and wiped clean two whole shelves. Even though it's a parent's job really.

Friday November 29th

8.50 a.m.
You're not going to believe this. I'd finished my history homework days ago (or Dad had, if you want to be boringly accurate) but I've still managed to forget it. I really did leave it on the kitchen table. Beachy Head is not going to be happy.

9.20 a.m.

We'd endured a whole school assembly (don't even ask me what it was about) and we were all surging off to lessons when I spotted of all people – my dad. He was looking a bit bewildered in the entrance when he spotted me and called, 'Hey, Louis, I come bearing homework!' He waved my history essay about, and then tore his way towards me through the hordes of pupils.

'Dad, you total star,' I said, grabbing the essay.

'I just spotted it on the table ...'

'You've saved my life.'

Dad looked around. 'I'd forgotten how big your school is.'

'Yeah, it's—' And that's when I gazed with undisguised horror and shock at the person lumbering our way. The one person I certainly didn't want Dad meeting. 'Well, I mustn't keep you,' I said, half pushing Dad towards the entrance. 'Looking quite a decent day outside' – it was bucketing down with rain – 'and you'll want to get some air now, won't you? You can't beat a bit of fresh air in your lungs, can you?'

I rambled on desperately, but it was too late. Beachy Head had sighted us. He half ran towards Dad, while I broke out in a sweat.

'Is this ... yes, you must be, Louis's father?' he

was spluttering with excitement.

'Dad was just leaving actually,' I cut in, 'because he's in a massive hurry.'

But Beachy Head didn't hear me. He was too busy shaking Dad's hand. 'I'm Mr Beach, the deputy head, and I'm very pleased to see you here.'

Beachy Head went on pumping Dad's hand as if he were his long lost brother, while Dad said, 'I was telling Louis that when I saw he'd forgotten his essay I tore up to the school, but was in two minds whether to come in—'

'Perfectly understandable,' interrupted Beachy Head.

'And I must have walked straight past Reception,' said Dad.

'Very easily done,' said Beachy Head. 'What's important is that you overcame those fears, didn't you?'

'Yes,' said Dad, his voice starting to fall away.

'And nothing you do in the future will be as hard as walking in here today. So, well done.'

'Thank you.' Dad's voice was growing even fainter.

'You know, seeing you here,' said Beachy Head, 'has made today so special for me.'

Now Dad was looking positively alarmed, while I was shaking with horror. If Dad found out I'd forged a letter to the school – let alone what I'd written about him – I'd be in deep, deep trouble.

'But we can't let a moment like this pass unnoticed,' said Beachy Head, showing Dad every one of his rotten teeth. 'How about a cup of coffee?'

My heart jumped into my mouth.

'No, I'd better go back ...' began Dad.

I nearly fainted with relief.

Beachy Head tapped Dad's hand. 'I completely understand. But the first step is always the hardest. Will you remember that?'

'I will,' said Dad softly.

'Well, next time drop in for that cup of coffee. And, congratulations again.'

As Beachy Head marched off, Dad shook his head. 'Wow, he's very friendly.'

'Very,' I agreed.

'And what was all that about the first step is always the hardest?'

'He likes to leave everyone with some wise words. It comes from doing so many assemblies, I suppose.'

'And why did he keep congratulating me?'

'He does that to everyone. Believes it builds a positive atmosphere.'

Dad shook his head. 'And I thought my

teachers had been eccentric.'

After Dad left I was still having trouble with my breathing. What a truly terrifying moment.

But I think I got away with it – for now!

Chapter Ten
Maddy's Veto

Saturday November 30th

9.40 a.m.
Mum was down early to cook breakfast and give us some decent food again (Dad's cooking hasn't improved). He said to Mum, 'The cleaning, the washing, the shopping and the cooking. Now I don't know how you did it all – and when you were working part time as well. And as soon as you clean something it is messy again.' Mum was nodding away now, 'while the loos are just gross to clean.'

'Hey, not when we're eating I growled.

'But haven't you found all this cleaning very

calming and relaxing?' asked Mum with a teasing smile.

Dad laughed a bit shame-faced then.

As Elliot and I were leaving, Mum called after us, 'Don't forget we shall want your help tomorrow lunch time.'

'Why, what's happening?' I asked.

'The neighbours are coming round. You remember, they invited your dad and me to their house last month ...'

'And you had a horrible time,' I said.

'Oh, I wouldn't say horrible,' said Mum.

'But you didn't like any of them. So now you're inviting them back. That definitely makes sense,' I said.

'They sort of invited themselves,' said Mum. 'So what could I say?'

'How about *no*,' I said.

'And what exactly have we got to do?' asked Elliot.

'Oh, nothing too strenuous,' began Mum. 'Just talk to them.'

Elliot and I groaned.

'And hand round plates of food,' went on Mum.

Elliot and I groaned again.

'And get dressed up in your best clothes,' added Dad, with a teasing smile.

'Stop I don't want to hear any more,' I said,

'as I frighten easily.'

'Are you paying us?' asked Elliot.

'I'll pretend I didn't hear that,' said Mum indignantly.

'That means they're not,' I said. 'It's pure child labour.'

11.50 a.m.

You'd be amazed how long it takes to write enough jokes to fill a three-minute act. But then I am being dead tough.

So here's a joke I've just rejected:

Why was the belt arrested?
Because it was held up.

That's just not funny enough for me. And I'm not sure about this one either:

What did one toilet say to the other?
You look a bit flushed.

But here's one I'm definitely keeping in:

What do you call a pig that can do karate?
A pork chop.

I'm smiling as I write that one down. I know I'll

love telling that joke.

12.05 p.m.
Just had a super-smart brainwave. You know I've got to give my act an extra twist. Well, here it is (get ready to be impressed).

Juggling.

So I'll be rattling off jokes, while at the same time expertly juggling apples and oranges and bananas. I've never done any juggling before, but how hard can it be? Plus, if I drop one I'll just laugh in a Tommy Cooper way as if to say, *That's part of the act.*

This is going to be so awesome.

12.11 p.m.
And I so want to dazzle Maddy tonight. I want her to have tears of laughter in her eyes as she whispers. 'How could I have dumped a boy who's such a marvellous joke-teller – and juggler?'

8.50 p.m.
When Maddy first came round it was spectacularly awkward. She was the colour of an over-ripe tomato, while my shoulders kept wobbling about all by themselves. But then, she is my first ever ex-girlfriend. So I was bound to feel a bit churned up inside when I met her

again. But I told myself, once I was joking and juggling, all our embarrassment will melt away.

But before we could go upstairs Mum appeared, her face one big smile.

'I just want you to know that I've heard about you and Louis.'

'Oh yes,' said Maddy gravely.

'And I'm just so happy. We both are,' Mum beamed.

Maddy gaped at her. Parents aren't usually so cheerful with girls who have recently dumped their sons.

'In fact, we've been smiling ever since Louis told us the news,' laughed Mum.

Maddy actually gasped now, while I thought, So Dad really has kept his promise to me – he hadn't breathed a word to Mum about Maddy and me breaking up. Who'd have thought it?

Upstairs Maddy said in this strange voice as if she'd just acquired a cold, 'Your mum's very happy about what's happened?' I was going to explain when Maddy went on, 'It is for the best, you know.'

And immediately I changed my mind. Instead, I started getting ready to perform my act. I arranged my selection of apples and oranges that I'd borrowed from downstairs. 'I think I know it off by heart already,' I explained, 'but

I've got my notes here, just in case.'

'Fine,' said Maddy relaxing a little. I took a couple of deep breaths and began.

Now I'll admit the juggling needed a bit more work, as I dropped, well, every one of the apples and oranges I'd borrowed from downstairs. But my jokes were ace.

Maddy really should have been laughing hysterically at them. Instead, not a flicker of a smile. She just sat there as lively as a pencil. And after I'd finished she didn't do anything as energetic as clap, no, she just went on sitting there. I've seen people in trances look more excited.

'Well, what's the verdict?' I asked, while giving an unusually nervous laugh. 'You look as if you're racking your brains for a compliment.'

'I am.'

'OK, well, I know the juggling needs a bit more work.'

'A bit!' she murmured.

'But the juggling was a good idea, wasn't it?' I asked eagerly.

Maddy pulled a face. 'Your juggling was just embarrassing. And you were concentrating so hard on that your timing was off on all your jokes.'

'That's a bit harsh,' I said, trying not to sound

too hurt.

She stood up, 'Louis, when you go on television you've got to give the biggest, best performance of your life.'

'You don't need to tell me that,' I said, a bit irritated by her tone. Then I added, 'If it eases your mind, I'm going to practise the juggling every single night.'

'It doesn't ease my mind at all,' she said. 'No, I'm sorry, Louis, but the juggling is definitely out. I'm using my veto on that.'

I stared at her. 'You're *what*?'

'As your agent I have the right of veto.'

'You've just made that up.'

'No, I haven't, and I'm using my right of veto now. The juggling is gone.'

Arguments are beyond me. I just don't do them. So even though I was very hurt by her negative attitude and irritated by all that veto rubbish, I said with a cheerful grin, 'I agree I need to do a lot more work on the juggling. So I'll juggle day and night and in my sleep and then let you see—'

'I shan't ever watch your juggling again,' Maddy announced dramatically. She was about to say something else when there was a knock on my bedroom door. Neither Maddy nor I had heard the doorbell, or Mum bringing our visitor upstairs.

'Here's Edgar,' began Mum a bit unnecessarily. Then, picking up on the tense atmosphere she went on, 'I'll leave you all to er – mingle. Let me know when you'd like some refreshments.'

Edgar – that jumped-up little geek – was someone I never wanted to see, but especially not now. And instantly the pleasantly stinky stench of my bedroom just gave up and expired, completely overtaken by Edgar's disgustingly clean freshly washed aroma. Still, ever the good host, I said, 'Hey, Edgar, you're very welcome, well, a bit welcome. What do you want anyway?

'Sorry to invade your sanctuary, but ...' He turned to Maddy. 'I have some very good news.'

'You're leaving the country,' I said.

'I am going to appear on television.'

'*Crimewatch*, is it?' I asked.

'I shall be on the local news programme in their Christmas special on December the thirteenth—'

'Not reading your Christmas poem?' interrupted Maddy excitedly.

'Yes, they liked my very wry look at the upcoming festivities. I've got to cut it down slightly, though.'

'Well, they want to keep some viewers,' I said.

'That's wonderful news!' cried Maddy, her eyes

91

all sparkling and lit up. And then she hugged Edgar right in the middle of my bedroom, which I thought was incredibly tactless and rude.

'I hope you didn't mind me appearing so unexpectedly,' said Edgar, with Maddy's arm still around him.

'Not at all,' I said. 'And if I were you I'd go on reading your poems on telly until everyone screams for mercy. Anyway, thanks for dropping by. Don't ever do it again.'

'I think we should go somewhere and celebrate,' said Maddy. 'I can pop back and help you later, Louis. You're re-working your act, aren't you?'

'No,' I said. 'Just polishing up my juggling.'

'Well then, I won't see you later,' said Maddy, looking daggers at me. It was only after they'd gone that I realized Edgar is going to be appearing on telly on exactly the same day as me – December 13th.

9.15 p.m.
It was bad enough Maddy dumping me – but now not laughing at my jokes? She knows how to wound.

She's still mad at me for calling her the Elephant Woman, isn't she? That's why she didn't smile once and made such a fuss about the juggling. Well, I'll show her. I'll be the slickest, fastest juggler there is.

9.40 p.m.
I was still practising my juggling when my parents trooped in. 'We're not being nosy or anything,' began Mum (which of course means they are), 'but things seemed a little strained between you and Maddy tonight.'

'Actually, you may as well know,' I said, perched on the end of my bed, 'but Maddy and I have split up. Well, she dumped me actually.' I briefly related the gory details.

'Why didn't you tell us before, you silly boy?' said Mum, sitting beside me on the bed. 'The more you bottle things up, the bigger they seem to be. That's right, isn't it?' She looked over at Dad, who was hovering by the door.

'Yes, quite right,' he agreed at once.

And then Dad gave me the tiniest wink. I doubt if it lasted for more than a millisecond. But somehow sharp-eyed Mum spotted it.

She shot up from my bed and pointed at Dad accusingly. 'You knew already, didn't you?'

Dad looked so embarrassed I wanted to laugh. 'I must admit I guessed, and then I asked Louis ...'

'Well, why didn't you say anything to me?'

93

demanded Mum.

'Because I asked Dad not to,' I said.

'Louis wasn't quite ready to tell you,' explained Dad.

'But he was ready to tell you,' said Mum. 'Well, I'm glad you've both finally agreed to let me in on the big secret.'

'It wasn't like that,' said Dad, moving over to her.

'It's only you've been incredibly busy lately,' I said, 'while Dad's just been hanging about all day, burning the toast.'

'You used to tell me everything,' said Mum.

'Mum, I'm a teenager now – you're lucky I talk to you at all.'

Mum gave a small smile then. 'Well, I'm glad you felt able to confide in one of us.'

'And Dad was really helpful,' I said, 'because he just talked to me normally.'

'I'm so happy about that,' said Mum, but she didn't sound very happy. Then she gave a gasp. 'When I said to Maddy tonight how pleased I was about you and her, she must have thought I was acting very strangely.'

'Don't worry, Mum,' I grinned. 'She thinks you're very strange anyway.'

Suddenly Mum looked at Dad and me as if we were two naughty boys. 'You two aren't hiding any more secrets from me, are you?'

Well, there was Dad doing all my homework. Mum definitely wouldn't approve of that. But we both just smiled innocently at her.

Sunday December 1st

11.05 a.m.
Mum and Dad are already tearing around tidying up the house. They're really kissing up to these neighbours, who they don't even like. Just tell me why?

11.50 a.m.
Elliot and me have been forced to wear our suits. Mum's also coached us on what to say when we're handing round the trays of food. 'You say, *please do help yourself.*'

'Let me write that down, Mum, before I forget it,' I said.

'We will also want you,' said Mum, 'to hand round some drinks.'

'Oh, big-time stuff.'

'And you can ask them polite questions, such as what their plans are for Christmas,' said Mum.

'But I really don't want to know,' I said.

'Yes, but you have to pretend you do,' said

Mum.

'Adults do a lot of pretending, don't they?' I said.

'And they should all be gone by two o'clock at the latest,' chipped in Dad.

'We'll all have died of boredom by then,' I said.

'Are you sure we're not getting paid?' asked Elliot.

1.10 p.m.

The neighbours were early. Twenty whole minutes early. And Mum and Dad had spent so much time making sure Elliot and I looked smart enough to breathe the same air as these neighbours, who they don't even like, that they weren't ready themselves.

'Boys,' called Mum, 'you'll have to open the door. Tell them we won't be long. Well, go on, hurry up.'

I bowed. 'Your humble servant, ma'am. Come on, Elliot – let's get ready for two hours of pretend smiling.'

'We should definitely get paid for doing this,' he muttered, thundering down the stairs after me.

There was such a fierce, icy wind outside that the four neighbours seemed to be blown into our house. First a tiny woman in a black and white polka-dot dress and with the most incredible blue hair I'd ever seen. She also had a blue ribbon in her hair, making her look exactly like an elderly, very sour-faced doll. Standing beside her was a large bear of a man in a tight-fitting brown suit.

And right behind them were Mr and Mrs Big Teeth. His front teeth were tremendous, and looked as if they were about to burst out of his mouth. He also clapped his hands when he said hello. (What do you bet he's always the first one to get up and dance at weddings?) He clearly thought he was a bit of a card. His wife was festooned in so many necklaces and bracelets I was surprised she didn't topple over under the weight of them all.

'Ah, you must be Elliot,' said Mrs Blue Hair to me, sounding as if she were the Lady Mayoress doling out the prizes.

'I'm Louis actually,' I said. 'The cool one. This is Elliot. But you can call him Little Legs.'

Elliot punched me and then grinned round at everyone like an over-friendly puppy.

'Oh yes, of course,' said Mrs Blue Hair vaguely. 'Well, it's nice to meet the young folk.' (She made us sound like leprechauns.) Then she started peering around. 'So where are your parents. Is everything all right?' she hissed conspiratorially.

'Totally fine. And Mum and Dad know you're swinging by and they'll be speeding down the stairs …' And at that moment, to my great relief, I saw Mum.

'I'm sorry,' said Mum to her guests.

'No, we're early,' cried Mrs Big Teeth.

'Yes, you are,' said Elliot loudly, and everyone looked at him for a moment. 'What did I say?' he whispered to me. 'They are early.'

And then another silence fell on everyone as Dad sauntered into view, a big smile plastered on his face. 'Hey, everyone, you're very welcome. How are you all?'

'More importantly,' said Mrs Big Teeth, 'how are you?' And she had this very concerned look on her face, as if she were visiting a sick invalid. 'We heard about' – her voice fell away – 'what happened to you.'

'Oh yeah, well, people get made redundant all the time now,' said Dad breezily.

'Can't be easy, though,' persisted Mrs Big Teeth.

Dad swallowed hard. 'It's a new adventure for us.'

'Just lucky your missus is able to keep the money rolling in,' said Mr Big Teeth with a flash of his pearly whites.

'Oh, it's quite common these days,' said Mum. 'Swapping roles for a while.'

'Is it really?' said Mrs Blue Hair. She couldn't have sounded more disbelieving if she'd tried. 'Well, it wouldn't work for us.' She looked at her husband. 'But then you keep getting promoted, don't you? In fact, your company would close down without you. So they'd never let you go.' Then they both gave Dad the biggest, smuggest smiles you've ever seen, as if to say: *Unlike you, you total loser.*

Here they were, the Blue Hairs and the Big Teeth, about to guzzle down free food and drink and all they could do was try and make Dad feel small.

That would have infuriated me anyway. But lately I'd spent so much time with Dad it was as if they were being nasty – well, to a mate of mine. And they didn't stop there. 'I'm sure the boys like seeing more of you,' said Mrs Big Teeth, 'though I expect they miss their mum.'

'Oh, they still see a lot of me,' said Mum crisply.

'Do they really?' murmured Mrs Big Teeth.

'And what does it matter who's paying the bills as long as someone is,' said Mrs Blue Hair.

The smile fell off Dad's face.

'And as you're the housewife now,' said Mr

Big Teeth, giving another of his unfunny laughs, 'we'll be inspecting your dusting later. We'll get my wife to give you marks out of ten. How about that?'

For a moment Dad had difficulty breathing. It was as if our guests had sucked all the air out of the room.

How dare these neighbours make fun of Dad? That was my job, not theirs – they were way out of order. Somehow Dad was keeping his cool. But I knew their snide little digs had really got to him.

I think Mum realized too as she jumped in, 'Well, what are we doing standing about in the hallway? Go and make yourselves comfortable in the sitting room. We'll bring some food and drink in to you – with the help of our crack team of young waiters here.'

In the kitchen Mum and Dad were quietly seething. But neither said a word. Mum just thrust trays of food at Elliot and me. 'Tell them we'll be in with more food and to sort out the drinks soon.'

But I hissed at Elliot in the hallway, 'Can you believe those neighbours?'

Elliot hissed back, 'I'd rather have four big fat snorting dinosaurs in my house than them. They're the stinkiest, stinky, rudest neighbours ever.'

'What are you waiting for, boys?' called Mum from the kitchen. 'Go and hand the food round.'

'We'll hand the food round, all right,' I whispered to Elliot. 'But I think it's time for our neighbours to get a bit of their own medicine.' I whispered to Elliot what I proposed to do. Then he couldn't stop laughing.

'Sssh,' I hissed. 'Mum and Dad mustn't have a clue what we're planning – though they'll thank us afterwards,' I added, a bit optimistically.

Chapter Eleven
My Invisible Friend

At first Elliot and me just handed round food, as we'd been told. Mrs Blue Hair surveyed my tray of savoury snacks apprehensively. 'Now we're not fussy eaters,' she said, 'but our stomachs can't cope with highly spiced food. So looking at what's there, no thanks. We have to watch our digestion, you see.'

'Well, maybe you'd just like some indigestion tablets,' I suggested brightly. 'I can bung a few on a plate for you ...'

'No, thank you,' she said firmly.

Then I gave Elliot our signal by nodding my head twice. My secret plan was to pay these neighbours back for being so mean to poor Dad by really embarrassing them in return. I hadn't a clue exactly what Elliot and I were going to do – I suppose if this were a lesson at school you'd call it Drama Improvisation.

Anyway, Elliot began the improvisation. He asked Mrs Big Teeth, 'Do you want to know what I've just done?'

'Yes, do tell me dear,' said Mrs Big Teeth, smiling indulgently. 'Children feel they can really open up to me,' she added to no one in particular. 'It's a little talent I have.' Elliot looked all around, as if unsure. Mrs Big Teeth's smile grew even soppier. 'Now, don't be shy, dear.'

Then he cried, 'I've just done a big poo and it was amazing.'

Mrs Big Teeth's eyes bulged and her jaw dropped in horror. The Blue Hairs' faces shrivelled with disgust.

'You're so lucky, Elliot,' I said, joining in. 'I haven't had a movement for four days. Still, when I do it'll be a real poo explosion.'

'And so stinky we'll have to open all the windows,' said Elliot. Then we both laughed very loudly while everyone just gaped at us.

'I really don't think this is a suitable topic for conversation,' said Mrs Blue Hair at last.

'But why not?' asked Elliot, with an innocent smile. 'We all do it, don't we?'

'Except me,' I said sadly. 'I feel so left out.' I turned to Mrs Blue Hair. 'So are you keeping regular?'

'Well, really,' began Mrs Blue Hair.

'Better change the subject, boys,' said Mr Big Teeth.

I nodded. 'I'm being very rude.'

'Yes, you are,' said Mrs Blue Hair firmly.

'Because I haven't introduced you to the other person who's here. I expect you're wondering who he is.'

The neighbours glanced round looking so puzzled I nearly burst out laughing. But it was vital I remained serious.

'There's no one else here,' said Mrs Blue Hair firmly.

'There is, actually, but he's a bit shy. He's hanging about in the doorway.'

The neighbours had drawn closer now as if banding together against this looney boy who kept seeing people who weren't there.

'Everyone,' I announced, 'meet Felix – my invisible friend.'

'Your what?' barked Mr Blue Hair.

But Mrs Big Teeth gushed delightedly in her tweety little voice. 'Children's games are such fun, aren't they?'

'Would you like to meet Felix?' I asked.

'Oh yes,' she cooed.

'Well, come forward.' I guided her into the middle of the room as if she were blindfolded. 'Felix is right in front of you.'

Mrs Big Teeth waggled her hands around. 'So happy—'

'I'm really sorry,' I interrupted. 'He's just walked away from you.'

'Oh,' Mrs Big Teeth actually sounded disappointed.

'I'll let you know if he comes back, though,' I said.

Suddenly Mr Blue Hair pointed a shocked finger at Elliot. 'What are you doing, lad?'

Elliot was, in fact, chewing his shirt. This was hilarious in the extreme and I was nearly proud of him. No wonder Mrs Big Teeth's eyes were popping out of her head like a snail's.

'I'm afraid he often does that,' I said quietly.

'But why?' asked Mr Big Teeth. 'Your dad's cooking isn't that bad, is it?' He laughed a bit desperately.

'This shirt doesn't taste as nice as the other ones,' wailed Elliot.

'The other ones,' repeated Mrs Big Teeth in a small, faraway voice.

'Yesterday he ate a whole candle,' I said.

'Loved that,' said Elliot, licking his lips

appreciatively before letting out a massive burp.

'This is a madhouse,' said Mrs Blue Hair in a piercing whisper to her husband. And that's when Mum and Dad bounced in with false smiles and bulging trays of cooked food.

'Sorry we were so long,' said Mum. 'Now I hope Louis and Elliot have been looking after you. Do tuck in.'

'And what would everyone like to drink?' asked Dad.

But no one answered. They all just stood there, wild-eyed with shock and horror.

'Have the boys have been entertaining you?' asked Dad.

Mrs Blue Hair snorted, while Mrs Big Teeth said softly, 'Louis's been introducing us to his invisible friend.'

'His what?' demanded Mum sharply. Then she gave me a look.

I knew it was time to go. 'Well, we'll leave you to have a good chat. Come on, Elliot – and Felix.'

There'd be a fall-out from all this, of course, but right then Elliot and I really didn't care. We'd paid the rancid old neighbours back for trying to humiliate Dad.

And upstairs Elliot and I just went on laughing and laughing. And somewhere I bet Felix was having a good giggle too.

Chapter Twelve

I Become a Swot (Temporarily)

1.45 p.m.

The neighbours were supposed to be cluttering up our house until two o'clock at least. Actually they'd all cleared off well before then. That looked like a result to me. And Mum and Dad should have been grateful to us.

But then Mum shrieked for Elliot and me to come downstairs. She didn't sound very grateful.

And she wasn't.

Mum and Dad stood facing us in the kitchen, grim and unsmiling.

Dad said gravely, 'We're not often ashamed

of you.'

'That's good to know,' I said.

'But today, with our guests,' thundered Mum, 'what got into you? I mean, all that total nonsense about an invisible friend?'

Elliot stifled a giggle.

'And then you,' said Dad to Elliot, 'started *eating your shirt.*'

'Awk – ward,' I trilled.

Elliot began to shake with silent laughter.

'And then you asked Mrs Adams if she was keeping regular?' said Mum.

'No, that was me, actually ...' I began. And then both Elliot and me burst out laughing. We just couldn't hold it in any more.

'This is *not* funny!' shouted Mum.

'Not funny at all,' agreed Dad. 'So stop laughing now.'

And finally Elliot and I managed to assume suitably solemn faces.

'After you left, the atmosphere was terrible,' said Mum.

'It was pretty awful before,' I said.

'You knew how important this little get-together was to your dad and me. And all we asked was that you were pleasant and polite,' said Mum.

'And if you couldn't say anything polite,' went

108

on Dad, 'don't say anything at all.'

'Just do mime, you mean,' I said.

'Louis,' cried Mum menacingly.

'Listen, Mum,' I explained, 'Elliot and I would have been the pleasantest, politest boys the world had ever seen if ...' I hesitated.

'If what?' asked Mum sharply.

'If they hadn't been so mean to Dad,' I said.

'They weren't exactly mean,' began Mum.

'Hey, Mum, they were.'

'They were meaner than dinosaurs,' added Elliot.

'That's what got us so mad,' I said quietly.

Dad looked right at Elliot and me for a second, and I thought he was about to say, 'Well done.' But instead he said, 'That is no excuse. You let us down today, boys.'

'And now go upstairs to your rooms,' ordered Mum, 'and think about your rudeness to our neighbours. You can only come down when you're sorry for what you've done.'

'We'll be up there a long time then,' I said.

'Sorry for not being sorry,' added Elliot.

As I was leaving I turned to Dad. 'They were only trying to make you look small, because they felt bad about themselves. So best to just ignore them and—'

'All right, Louis,' interrupted Mum.

But Dad looked amazed by what I'd just spouted. For a boy who's bottom of the class in everything I can be surprisingly full of wisdom sometimes.

6.20 p.m.
Really terrible storm here this afternoon. It even blew our aerial down, so cutting us off from civilization for a while.

The wind was still throwing all its sound effects at us when Dad went out to try and put the aerial back. He called upstairs to Elliot and me – who were still banished to our rooms – to come and help. Dad climbed up the ladder which Elliot and I held (and it was really swaying about). It took him a while, but finally Dad slotted it back.

No time to celebrate, though, for Mum had been rung up by this neighbour she visits – a very old lady called Mrs Gladwell to say her TV aerial was down too. So Dad, Elliot and me – and our trusty ladder – visited her house for another successful mission.

Mrs Gladwell said she was so grateful to us, as now she wouldn't miss *Antiques Roadshow*, and she fed us thousands of jam tarts and sausage rolls.

I was actually disappointed no one else

wanted their TV aerials put back. And I think Dad was too, as he kept on saying how the three of us made a good team. And neither he nor Mum mentioned again what had happened at lunch time.

Monday December 2nd

12.30 p.m.
Beachy Head has just returned the history essays. He made me come up to the front of the class. I thought Dad had messed up somehow – well, he was a bit out of practice. But then I opened my exercise book and was totally dazzled by what I saw.

A letter I've never seen anywhere near my work before.

An A gleamed and glistened and glowed. And I just felt so proud.

All right, I hadn't actually written a single word of it – but I'd copied it superbly. That had to count for something. And Dad and I shared the same genes. So it was all in the family, wasn't it?

Beachy Head said to me, 'You've really got to grips with this subject, haven't you?'

I struggled to look intelligent. Not easy for me.

He continued, 'Your analysis of the world situation was especially penetrating.'

'Yes, well, I'm very interested in the situation in the world. It's just so … interesting.' My voice fell away. Even I didn't know what in the name of Father Christmas I was rambling on about.

But still, I'd got an A. I'm a swot. And those are two sentences I never thought I'd write.

5.10 p.m.
When I got home, Dad was on Skype talking and laughing with this smart-looking guy I didn't recognize. Good to see Dad chilling with his mates, I thought.

But afterwards he didn't look very chilled.

'Who was that?' I asked.

'A guy I used to employ,' muttered Dad. 'I thought he might want to return the favour.'

I was stunned. 'You're going back to work now?'

'Oh yes,' said Dad. 'This set-up was only temporary.' That was news to me.

'So is Mum coming back home …?'

'No, no, we'll probably get someone in part time,' he said vaguely.

'And when are you going to work for the guy on Skype?' I asked.

Dad frowned. 'He'd really love to have me

on his team. But right now he's constrained by budgets.'

'Still, it's good he'd love to have you on his team,' I said, keen as always to highlight the bright side.

Dad nodded, but he still looked like the saddest person in the world.

But I knew how to bring the sunshine back into his life.

'Feast your eyes on this.'

'What is it?' began Dad. Then he saw that A and just forgot all about that guy on Skype. 'We got an A?' he said.

'We sure did, Dad.'

'And no one else got an A for this essay. Just us! Beachy Head said it was a particularly challenging topic too.'

'I was worried my style might have been a bit out of date,' said Dad, 'as I haven't written an essay like that for years.'

'No, you've still got it, Dad,' I said. And he looked so chuffed I even felt a little warm glow inside. Then I asked, 'How are you at French and English?'

'Pretty good, I think,' said Dad.

I left the homework details invitingly on the table.

7.02 p.m.

Tonight Dad served up a dodgy stew. He said he had got the recipe off the Internet. He seemed to have chucked everything into it, including some of his toenail clippings. 'Who says I can't dish up an appetizing meal?' said Dad.

'Us,' Elliot murmured, after he'd eaten the first mouthful. Then he looked at me for backup.

Elliot was right – it was totally inedible. But I felt an odd kind of loyalty to Dad these days. So I managed to swallow down a few mouthfuls. It was like eating thick medicine – only not so tasty.

Then Dad told us he had batch-cooked it – so there was tons more of it! A shudder of total horror ran through all three of us.

'I'm going to waste away and die of starvation then,' whispered Elliot.

And Mum piped up, 'I think you might have overcooked it very slightly.' It is the first time she has criticized any of Dad's cooking. 'So maybe we could have something different tomorrow?'

Dad just nodded glumly. I think he is totally sick of cooking and of housework and shopping – all of it. He still does it all, but not with the wild enthusiasm he used to display. Now when he's cleaning something he's got this faraway look in his eyes. The identical expression I have in all my lessons actually. Still, he'll be back at work any day now.

Tuesday December 3rd

6.45 p.m.
Dad announced tonight, 'I have prepared a rare delicacy for you all. Something very special.'

Elliot sniggered.

'I just hope I haven't scorched it too much.'

'Which means he has,' hissed Elliot.

But then Dad served up beans on toast, while laughing in such an odd way neither Elliot nor I said a word.

Finally Mum jumped up. 'Beans on toast – what a marvellous choice, so nutritious. I'll just chop up some salad to go with it.'

8.10 p.m.
Had a very odd text from Maddy – her first since Saturday night.

Have you dropped the juggling yet? That was all she said.

I texted back equally briefly: **No I haven't as I'm improving all the time.**

That will show her, I thought. She was a total nightmare on Saturday night, sitting there all stony-faced and spouting that rubbish about having a veto. Well, now I've put her in her place.

8.30 p.m.
You won't believe what Maddy's done now.
Well, read it for yourself.

Louis, you have changed. You have become very big-headed and do not listen to me any more. So I shan't be going with you to the TV studio on December 13th. I shall be accompanying my other client instead.
I shall try and remember the good times.
Maddy

8.34 p.m.
Just as I am about to step into the jaws of fame Maddy throws a strop – and over nothing.

8.50 p.m.
Here's my remarkably restrained reply.

I am extremely sorry you won't be going with me on the 13th December. But, Maddy, I haven't changed – you have.
I will also try and remember the good times.
Louis

Chapter Thirteen
Maddy to the Rescue

Wednesday December 4th

I've made a new mate.

Like me, he's got an onion-shaped head and his ears stick out exactly the same as mine too. But he is blond-haired, with very dark eyes, and more importantly he's hilarious. In fact, he's nearly as funny as me. He has got just this one tiny, little flaw.

He's imaginary.

Still, nobody's perfect, are they? His name is Felix, by the way. That's right – he's the imaginary friend I made up for our neighbours. Well, he's back, livening up all my lessons.

You're starting to worry about me now, aren't you? Well, don't. I'm not setting a place for Felix next to me, or walking along the road chatting to him. And I do know he just lives inside my head and is realistically challenged. (Felix prefers that to being called imaginary.)

Thursday December 5th

A teacher smiled at me in the corridor today. That's a rare historical event, I can tell you. Mrs Mack, the English teacher said, 'Louis, I've just read your essay on *An Inspector Calls*, and for the first time I feel as if I might have taught you something.' Then she practically danced off to her next lesson. Dad taking over my homework has cheered her up no end.

Friday December 6th

7.00 p.m.
Only one week to go until *Kids with Attitude*. So I've just performed my act for Felix.

And he didn't smile once.

When you can't even amuse your imaginary (sorry, realistically challenged) friend, you're in massive trouble, aren't you?

It's not fair either, because I practised

the juggling all week. But you know what, I'm still rubbish. I see it now. And Maddy is right. There's a sentence I hated writing. But she is. And my act is a complete and total DISASTER.

What can I do?

7.09 p.m.
When Gotham City was in trouble, Chief Commissionaire Gordon would send Batman a message in the sky. Me, I pick up my mobile and call ... Maddy.

7.10 p.m.
She might put the phone down on me. Well, if she does, I'll just keep on trying. I've never needed her help more urgently than now.

7.14 p.m.
Maddy didn't put the phone down on me. Not that I gave her much chance. As soon as she picked up I gabbled, 'I've just got one word to say to you, Maddy. Sorry. And I'll go on saying it until you get bored. Sorry, sorry, sorry, sorry, sorry ... are you getting bored yet?'

'No, not yet,' said Maddy. She sounded a tiny bit amused.

'OK, I'm sorry, sorry, so sorry, incredibly

sorry. Amazingly sorry ... I'll even sing it if you like.'

And I started, 'Maddy, I'm very, very sorry ...'

'Oh stop,' she cried, 'you've got a terrible singing voice. But what exactly are you sorry about anyway?'

'My juggling.'

'Oh, right. You know, I so wish I still didn't have a picture of you juggling in my head.'

'And I can totally see why. I'm the worst juggler in the world, aren't I?'

'Without a doubt.'

'But I thought ... I don't know what I thought. But my whole act is in tatters now. And in only a week's time I'm appearing on television, in the biggest chance of my life. Maddy – can you come round?'

'When?

'Now.'

'OK,' she said, and put the phone down.

7.25 p.m.

No superhero could have moved much faster than Maddy. She was round my house before I knew it.

'Thanks a billion for this,' I said.

'I wasn't doing much,' she replied.

Upstairs I explained. 'Right up until tonight,

you know I still thought my act was ace—'

'So what happened tonight?' interrupted Maddy.

'Felix didn't laugh at all.' The name had slipped out before I realized it.

And Maddy was on to it right away. 'Who's Felix?'

'That's a good question and I'll answer it immediately,' I began, before stopping completely.

'Come on, tell me,' she persisted.

'All right, he's sort of a boy in my class, but in another way he isn't because I can see him but no one else can.'

For the first time tonight Maddy was looking right at me. 'You mean he's imaginary?'

'You might well call him that – yes.'

She was positively staring at me now. 'And you talk to him.'

'Not out loud, I'm not a total loon.' I laughed a bit uncertainly. 'But in my head I kind of hear him. He's dead funny, actually.'

'Is he?' said Maddy softly. She was actually smiling now. 'Have you had an imaginary friend before?'

'Never, and I've only had him since Wednesday really. He just appeared at school and we hit it off. What am I talking about? Anyway, you don't want to hear about him.'

'Yes I do,' said Maddy.

'Look, I'm not going off my onion or anything.'

Maddy stood up. 'You talk to him and he talks back?'

'I know he doesn't really,' I said, a bit defensive now. 'But forget about him.'

'No, I won't,' said Maddy, looking excited suddenly, 'because he's *it*.'

I still didn't get what she was talking about.

Her voice rose. 'He's going to make your act special, as you will be the first-ever comedian to share the stage with an imaginary mate.'

'But no one else will see him,' I said.

'That doesn't matter, as the audience will see him through your eyes. You'll tell them what he's saying.' She paused. 'You say he's funny?'

'Well, I think he is.'

'Brilliant. You can tell jokes together. So now I just want you to do your old act but with interruptions from Felix.' She went on, 'Talk in your normal voice but then have Felix trying to take over. And make sure Felix sounds completely different to you as well ... Can you do impressions?'

'I do a mean Captain Jack Sparrow.'

'Well, now Felix sounds exactly like him,' she said.

So I rattled off a few jokes as usual. Then I yelled out in my best Captain Jack Sparrow voice, 'Felix here, Louis's realistically challenged mate. How do you cure a headache? *Put your head through a window and the pane will just disappear.*' Then when I saw Maddy really laughing, I said in my normal voice, 'Hey, you're not laughing more at Felix's jokes than mine, are you?'

'That's funny,' cried Maddy. 'Keep it in. And I love Felix's voice by the way. Perfect.'

So I carried on, with me telling a couple of jokes and then Felix bursting in and trying to top it with one of his own.

I know it sounds crazy.

It *is* crazy.

But it really did work. It was fresh and different – and funny. When I finished, Maddy didn't say anything at first. Then she said slowly, 'Now, Louis, I really think you could win next week.'

Chapter Fourteen

Exposed

Saturday December 7th

5.20 p.m.
Dad won't be at home all day much longer, as he's had a call today from an old mate who wants to meet with him on Monday afternoon. Dad's mad keen to show this guy his ideas and has spent all day working on a PowerPoint presentation and is in an alarmingly happy mood.

I'm pleased for Dad. But I hope he remembers he's still got responsibilities at home – like doing my homework.

* * *

Sunday December 8th

Maddy has just heard my act again. She laughed even more than last time. Even her eyebrows were dancing with delight.

I said, 'It's just a shame you're not coming with me on Friday.'

'But I've promised Edgar ... and he's reading two poems aloud now.'

'Sounds like a magical evening ... I just wish you were—'

'No, Louis, don't even ask me.'

And with that she left.

Monday December 9th

2.40 p.m.

Had two free lessons today, as tons of people – including some teachers – are away with this tummy lurgie, which is racing round the school. Beachy Head was still there, though, worse luck. I don't suppose any germs could smuggle through his beard.

Still, the good news was that Dad and me got another A in history today. The not so good news was that after giving the homework back, Beachy Head announced that we were having a surprise test. And I could hardly answer any of it.

Still, I have learned an important lesson. Blinded by my desire for academic glory, I let Dad do my essays too well. I'll have to make sure I don't get any higher than a C in future.

So how am I going to explain getting an A at home and a Z in the test? But maybe Beachy Head won't mark the tests straight away. I might even be discovered on television before he reads my miserable offering.

Or, of course, Beachy Head could do the decent thing and catch the tummy lurgie. Here's hoping.

5.10 p.m.
When I got home I thought I'd have the house to myself for once, with Mum at work, Elliot rehearsing *Oliver*, and Dad dazzling an old mate with all his ideas. I was pleased to have all this free time, though oddly not quite so pleased as I'd expected. I suppose I'd got used to Dad haunting the house when I came home.

But anyway, I'd just shut the door when a deeply grumpy voice called out, 'Must you slam the door when you come in? You made all the windows rattle.'

I was shocked. First of all, by this slur on my door-closing abilities. Everyone knows that if the windows shake a bit that's a good sign as it means the door is well and truly shut. But also that Dad was home already. Then he emerged. Gloom dripping off him. He just nodded at me and then wandered off again.

I sensed that his meeting had not gone well, because I'm quick like that. So I did something for him which I normally only do on Father's Day. I made him a cup of tea. Not only that, I put out four chocolate digestives (his favourites) on a plate. I even carried the tray over to where he was slumped in the sitting room.

'Afternoon tea, sir,' I said. 'Compliments of the management. There's no charge, but tips are always extremely welcome.' Then I plonked down beside him. 'I'm only guessing here, but it looks as if this geezer wasn't wild about your ideas.'

'I never had a chance to show him anything.' And Dad was practically frothing with anger. 'I was in and out of there in twenty minutes. He said he only wanted to touch base with me. But really he was just going through the motions.'

'And he didn't offer you anything?'

'He said he'd like to but he was afraid I was over-experienced ...' Dad gave a deep sigh. 'They know when you're struggling.'

Was that what Dad was doing – struggling? I suppose it was.

'And they immediately start to treat you differently, belittle you. That's how I felt today, belittled and shut out.'

Dad was really opening up to me. I struggled to think of something intelligent to say.

'Well, it's that geezer's loss, Dad, because you're brilliant. I know that because – well, look at this. You've only gone and got another A in history.' I slapped the exercise book down on the table. Dad snatched it up, stared at the grade and Beachy Head's rave review. 'I mean, I'd have been happy with a C,' I said, 'or a D, come to that. My standards are very low but my gratitude is immense. Dad, you've transformed me into Super Swot. Now I can look teachers in the face without shrieking in terror. Never happened to me before. And all thanks to you, Super Brain.'

Dad looked at me for a moment and then put his head back and really laughed. See, I know how to cheer him up. Then he asked, 'So what homework have we got tonight?' I ate the four chocolate digestives while Dad got down to work.

Tuesday December 10th

5.30 p.m.
I was a bit late tonight. And when I got home

Dad was staring out of the front window, waiting for me. Again. But it really doesn't bug me like it used to. In fact, it seems almost normal now.

Anyway, he was all excited because he'd been sorting out the loft and discovered another photograph album he'd forgotten about. 'Back in those far-off days, when we took pictures not with our phones but with an invention you probably haven't heard of called the camera,' he grinned.

Now I'm never happier than when looking at Dad and his mates, all with tragic 1987's hairstyles, squashed around a table, then squashed around another table and then – yeah, you guessed it, yet another one.

'Doesn't time fly,' said Dad, staring into the pictures and shaking his head.

'Not right now it doesn't,' I murmured.

And then Dad dug out some pictures of himself dancing. Now they were fascinating in a grizzly sort of way. 'So what are you doing there?' I asked.

'What are we doing?' cried Dad indignantly. 'People travelled for miles to see Lee and me do the moonwalk.'

'I'd travel for miles not to see you,' I said.

'Well, I bet you can't do the moonwalk,' challenged Dad.

'I bet I can.' I jumped up. The moonwalk is actually the easiest dance in the world, as I very quickly demonstrated. Or thought I had.

'No, all wrong,' said Dad getting up. 'You've got to put all your weight on the foot you're keeping still, while sliding the other one backwards on the heel. The big secret is keeping the heel on the ground at all times. Look, watch.'

Dad's dancing is not a sight for the sensitive. But I swallowed hard and even encouraged him until he demanded, 'Now do it with me.'

In a list of uncool things to do in the afternoon, performing a cheesy dance with your dad would be right up there at the top, wouldn't it?

But then I thought, Here's Dad stuck at home on his own and abandoned by just about every one of his mates, so if performing the moonwalk with his offspring helps to cheer him up – I'll do it. I suppose the best word to describe me is heroic.

8.30 p.m.

Only three days to go until the *Kids with Attitude* Final now. Been practising all the time. And Evie has just called with the final arrangements. A car will be picking up Dad and me at the house at 4.00 p.m. sharp. We rehearse at 5 p.m. Then the show goes out totally live at 7.00 p.m.

Mum and Dad were quite surprised when they found out Maddy wasn't going with me. 'A clash of clients,' I said, and quickly changed the subject. I'm still hoping Maddy might change her mind at the last moment. But it doesn't seem very likely.

Wednesday December 11th

12.15 p.m.

More teachers have gone down with this stomach bug – but not Beachy Head. I've just passed him lurking around the corridor like a deadly shark. I kept my head down and tried to slip past him, but I must have one of those very noticeable personalities as he suddenly loomed over me.

I knew right away he'd marked my test as it took him about a year to stop frowning.

'What happened, Louis?'

I struggled to think of a reason.

'You've been writing so well.' He shook his head. 'But in the test I did think you had a preoccupied look.' That was me trying to find a question I could answer. He lowered his voice. 'Your father – he hasn't had a relapse?'

I leaped on this. 'Yeah, that's exactly what he's had.'

'I feared this might happen.'

'It's just a tiny little relapse, but I couldn't stop thinking about it all during the exam.'

Beachy Head patted my shoulder. 'You mustn't worry, Louis.'

'I'll try not to.'

Then he swept off, while I let out the largest sigh of relief you've ever heard. I'd got away with it. And once I win *Kids with Attitude* on Friday, school will be a thing of the past anyway.

I'll probably never ever see Beachy Head again.

5.45 p.m.

Something truly, truly terrible has just happened.

Hello again, Louis

Chapter Fifteen

I'm in Very Deep Trouble

5.45 p.m. (cont'd)

It happened right out of the blue as well.

When I got home Dad had just finished sorting out the garden for the winter (whatever that means) and was having a shower. He shouted down to me to put the kettle on. Then the doorbell rang.

I casually opened the door and then I saw something so awful I closed and unclosed my eyes, in the desperate hope that it would go away.

But Beachy Head was still standing there.

'Howarrh,' I spluttered – I was so shocked I made up a new word! But I was angry too. How dare he turn up at my house? He didn't belong in this world.

'Hello again, Louis.' He was wearing the same suit as at school and had the same battered case he always carried about with him. 'Is your father about?'

I knew of course that this was one meeting which really couldn't happen. Clutching at the door handle to steady myself, I tried to think fast. I lowered my voice. 'Dad's, er, resting at the moment, and I don't like to disturb him,' I added confidingly. 'I'm afraid it's not one of his better days.'

'I see. Well, is your mother around?'

'Oh no, still at work. Won't be back for hours yet, but I can take a message. I'm very good at taking messages.'

Beachy Head hesitated. But then Dad called down the stairs, 'Who is it?'

And quick as a flash Beachy Head called back, 'It's Mr Beach, and I would greatly appreciate a word with you.'

'I'll be right down,' said Dad. And he was, in his dressing gown. 'Forgive me for not being properly dressed ...' he began.

'Do not worry, I completely understand,'

interrupted Beachy Head with a sickly smile.

'I've been in the garden.'

'So you've been outside anyway,' said Beachy Head. 'Well, that's encouraging. And maybe tomorrow you might go for a walk.'

'Yes, I might,' said Dad faintly. 'Er, would you like to come in?'

As Beachy Head pounded into the sitting room, he gave me a look. And I knew exactly what it meant. He wanted me to leave them alone. But no way was I doing that. So instead I sat right beside my teacher. He sat down opposite Dad and spoke to him in a low whisper, 'Just to let you know, my brother-in-law had the same little problem as you. But he has fully recovered now.'

Dad was gazing at Beachy Head more and more warily. 'What little problem is that?'

'I think you know,' said Beachy Head just a trifle impatiently.

'No, I'm sorry, I don't.'

'Ah well, what does it matter,' I said cheerily. 'Going to be Christmas before we—'

'Oh, you mean about me ...' Dad interrupted.

'Exactly,' said Beachy Head.

'Exactly,' I said, desperate to change the subject. 'So that's all sorted out.'

'But how do *you* know about that?' Dad asked Beachy Head, looking puzzled and a bit cross.

'You told me.'

Dad gaped at the deputy head. '*I* told you.'

'Yes, you wrote me a letter explaining your situation.'

'I don't remember that,' said Dad.

'But you've had a lot on your mind, Dad.' I got up. 'Anyway, have you put your Christmas decorations up yet, Mr—'

'Just a second, Louis,' interrupted Dad. 'I wrote you a letter, Mr Beach?'

'And I'm so glad you did,' said Beachy Head, 'because it helped me understand Louis. He has taken a little while to settle in, but lately I've taken him under my wing, you might say.' He smiled proudly at me. 'And he's blossomed, produced some really outstanding work.'

'Oh, I wouldn't go that far,' I began ... then my voice fell away. Just when I thought things couldn't get any worse I heard Mum's car pull up. The very last thing I wanted was her joining in this conversation.

Beachy Head was still holding forth to Dad about how it would be a good idea if they put their heads together – so I slipped outside for a moment.

Mum was getting stuff out of the boot of her car. I raced over to Elliot. 'Mum mustn't go inside yet,' I hissed at him.

'Why not?' he asked, not unreasonably.

'No time to explain, just do something, anything, but keep her out here, until I give you the signal.'

In moments of crisis – and this was certainly one of them – Elliot and I temporarily forget all our many differences. So I knew I could trust him to do something.

I tore back indoors – and then the most blood-curdling howl you've ever heard just erupted. I tell you, it made all the hounds of the Baskervilles sound like amateurs. Dad sped to the front door while Beachy Head tottered to his feet. 'What on earth was that?'

'Just my little brother,' I said.

'Does he make that noise often?' he asked.

'Oh, he's usually much louder than that. This is one of his quieter days … welcome to my family.' I rushed on, 'Sorry about Dad's memory lapse, but now's not a good time for us.'

'Yes, I can see that,' said Beachy Head, who had a dazed – you might even say, shattered – look about him now. 'I think it might be better if I spoke to you tomorrow at school where things are calmer.'

Relief swept over me. 'Yes it would.' We'd reached the door. 'Well, it's been a pleasure seeing you,' I lied.

Mum and Dad both had their arms around Elliot who was yelling, 'This toothache, it's just terrible!' And they were concentrating so hard on Elliot they hardly noticed Beachy Head until Mum looked up and stared for a moment at the unfamiliar figure leaving the house.

'It's Mr Beach, isn't it?' she said.

'That's right, Mum,' I said quickly. 'He just popped by, but now he's got to rush off.'

'Good afternoon,' he said politely to Mum.

And I really think the old gargoyle would have gone if Dad hadn't called out, 'I never wrote you a letter, you know.'

'What letter?' demanded Mum at once.

'Dad's forgotten about a letter he wrote,' I said. 'But it's no biggie. I'm far more worried about Elliot. Are you in a lot of pain?'

I signalled at my brother to do some wailing and fast, but he was too fascinated by what Beachy Head did next. He reached into his pocket and then called out, 'Actually, I brought the letter you wrote with me.'

'Well, we're all too anxious about Elliot to read it now,' I said.

But Dad, moving forward, asked, 'May I see it please?' He took it, then started to read it and immediately the colour began to drain from his face. Finally he said quietly, 'I think we should

138

all go back inside.'

We all filed into the sitting room. Mum quickly read the letter too, then gave me a most unfriendly look and turned to Elliot. 'How's your toothache?' she asked. 'You know, I wouldn't be surprised if it disappeared as suddenly as it appeared.'

'Well, it's not quite so bad,' admitted Elliot.

'Louis asked you to pretend to be ill, didn't he?' Before Elliot could reply, she said, 'Just go upstairs. We'll deal with you later.'

After Elliot left I said hopefully, 'If I'm in the way I can leave too.'

'You stay there,' growled Mum. She seemed to be taking charge of things now, while Dad hovered about looking as if he'd just been bitten on the leg.

Then Mum demanded, 'You wrote this letter, didn't you, Louis?'

'Me? What an accusation! Well, maybe, quite possibly, but I'll have to consult my lawyer before I say anything else.'

'Perhaps you'd also like to see the letter *I* sent *you*,' purred Beachy Head, 'as I have also brought that with me.'

He would!

He produced the letter with something of a flourish, and Mum and Dad, who were now standing closer together than Siamese twins, quickly scanned its contents. Then they turned their scorching gaze onto me.

'Why didn't you show this letter to us?' demanded Dad.

That was easy: I didn't want anything to jeopardize me appearing on *Kids with Attitude*. But if I admitted that now, it might encourage my parents to do the very thing I feared most. So I babbled, 'I didn't want to worry you, as you both had a lot on your minds already, and well, you know how soft-hearted I am ...'

The door opened. 'Can I come in and just listen?' asked Elliot.

'No, go back upstairs at once,' snapped Mum.

Elliot scarpered.

Mum, who was quivering now like a volcano due to explode any second said, 'I'm very sorry about this, Mr Beach. You can rest assured we will deal with it.'

'Forging a letter from a parent is a very serious business,' said Mr Beach.

'But it is my first offence,' I murmured. 'Well, I think it is ...'

Beachy Head went on, 'I believed this letter was genuine, and its unusual style was because of personal problems. So I have helped Louis.'

'We're very grateful,' murmured Mum.

I wasn't.

'And I had been pleased to note a marked improvement in his history homework,' continued Beachy Head. 'Some of his recent essays have been outstanding.'

A little gleam of pride crossed over Dad's face. Unfortunately Mum spotted it too, and then looked accusingly at me.

'But his history exam result was very disappointing. I wondered at first if fresh worries at home might have caused such a marked deterioration. Now I fear there may be another explanation.'

'So do I,' said Mum, darting a glance at Dad. 'Perhaps you will be kind enough, Mr Beach, to leave this matter to us to sort out too.'

After Beachy Head had finally lumbered off, Mum turned accusingly to me. 'We're disgusted.'

'So am I,' I said. 'He just turns up and crashes in here uninvited.'

'With you,' snarled Mum.

'Why did you do it, Louis?' Dad sounded really puzzled.

'Can I have an easier question?' I quipped.

They both shook their heads at me. Then Mum hissed, 'What also makes me angry is the way you've taken advantage of your father.'

I stared at her. 'What do you mean?'

'You know,' said Mum.

'No, I don't, as actually, Mum, I'm the one who's been cheering Dad up. I even did the moonwalk with him yesterday. How many teenage sons can say the same?'

'I mean, persuading your poor dad to do all your homework.'

'I didn't persuade him. He wanted to do it – didn't you, Dad?'

'Thank you for remembering I'm still here,' said Dad.

'I'm sorry, love,' said Mum, 'but Louis's obviously been running rings round you. And that makes me furious on your behalf.' Then she asked him if he'd done any other homework for me apart from history.

That's when Dad admitted he was in fact a serial homework doer. 'I thought,' he explained, 'that if I help Louis lift his grades that will give him the confidence to take over later.'

Mum shook her head very doubtfully, then said gently to Dad, 'But he's not learning anything, love.'

'Yes, I am,' I announced loudly.

'What?' demanded Mum. And Dad turned hopefully towards me.

'I'm learning that Dad's much better at doing my homework than me.' I grinned.

Mum snorted contemptuously and Dad actually turned away from me. 'Not everything is funny, Louis,' said Mum.

Well, if it isn't, it should be. And I really didn't see what was wrong with trying to inject a little hilarity into the grim proceedings.

'I blame myself,' said Mum.

'Fair enough,' I agreed.

Positively glaring at me now, Mum went on. 'I've been busy lately with so many new responsibilities. And I did think I could rely on my oldest son to rally round your dad and help him, but instead ... Oh, get out of my sight. You can wait in your bedroom until we have decided your punishment.'

I'm still waiting.

6.59 p.m.

Actually seeing Mum, and especially Dad, look so hurt at what I'd done ... and so bitterly disappointed in me ... well, believe me that's a punishment in itself. And remorse has shot through me more than once.

But what my parents don't realize is that it's very tough being an undiscovered comedy icon, with a life-changing opportunity fluttering in the wings. I'm under a lot of pressure just now. And they should make allowances for that, shouldn't they?

7.10 p.m.
Mum and Dad (well, mainly Mum) have just gone sensationally ballistic. They ranted on and on about how I'd crossed a line this time, while I looked dead sorry and nodded a lot. They said I had to write a letter of apology to Beachy Head. 'And we've told him,' added Mum, 'that we will agree with whatever punishment the school wants to give you.'

'Cheers for that,' I murmured.

And I'm to be grounded until the New Year! After they said that, I felt my entire life come crashing down around me. Just hours before my appointment with destiny – *Kids with Attitude* – they were going to pull the plug on it.

Well, I wouldn't let them. Somehow I'd escape. But then Mum announced there would be just one exception ... *Kids with Attitude*. 'As I'd worked so hard for that.'

'A squillion, gazillion thanks,' I murmured. I was really grateful and I smiled at them both.

'Have you got any questions?' asked Dad.

'Yeah, will I be allowed to pop out and see Father Christmas?'

I waited for Dad to laugh. I'd got him smiling so many times over the past few weeks. Only yesterday he'd really roared with laughter at my antics. But tonight, when I so needed a brief moment of friendliness, not a flicker. In an instant Dad has abandoned me and gone all serious and boring and grown-up.

He just said, 'You've really let yourself down today.' Then he added, before turning away from me, 'And you've let me down.' He didn't say you've let *us* down. He said *me*. As if I'd done something especially bad to him.

All right, I'd made one big mistake. I shouldn't have forged that letter and I'm truly very sorry, blah, blah, blah. But every afternoon since time began – or so it seems – I've been talking to my dad. And not just the normal grunts most teenager boys reward their parents with. No, I've had proper, long conversations with him about everything under the sun.

I've never spoken so much to anyone, ever – not even Maddy. And if they knew on Twitter what I'd done, I bet they'd be nominating me for some kind of award now.

Best son of the year or something like that.

And even letting Dad do my homework was a sort of good deed really. The way his face just lit up when he got those A grades.

But that's all gone up in smoke now. And Dad hadn't even tried to defend me tonight. Instead, he's morphed from my mate into this unsmiling adult who says I've let him down. Well, fine – I think he's let me down too.

So we're equal.

Chapter Sixteen

A Top Secret Disaster

Thursday December 12th

4.10 p.m.

When I got home tonight Mum was there too. She said she'd managed to finish early, and she was bustling about the house taking charge again. Dad just sat frowning at his laptop.

Mum asked me what punishment I'd got at school for my spell of forgery. I told her I'd been given a lecture from Beachy Head which lasted several thousand years, and multiple detentions, starting on Monday.

'Excellent,' said Mum, which I think is a very poor attitude for a parent and a weaker person than myself would be quite hurt by her mean opinion of me.

Then I said to Dad, 'Only a week until the end of term and they're still setting us homework. Can you believe that?'

I thought such tragic news might stir him into offering to help me at least. But he just said, 'You'd better get on with it, then,' in a voice dryer than the Sahara desert.

'OK, I will do my homework all by myself and completely not helped by anyone. Just call me swotty knickers,' I added with a winning smile.

But Dad didn't smile back.

5.10 p.m.

I've actually taken out my homework and stared at the questions. I so wished I could answer them, just to show my dad I didn't need him.

But I couldn't.

Then Maddy rang and asked how I was feeling. At last, a question I could answer.

'Dead excited about tomorrow but hating tonight. The atmosphere is so bad it's made every room seem miserable – even my bedroom.'

That's why I've told Maddy not to come round. She was planning to hear me perform my act with Felix one last time.

'No comedian could be funny in this house

tonight,' I said. 'And I'm not allowed to leave it either.'

'Poor Louis,' she said quite softly. 'I will be keeping everything crossed for you tomorrow, you know.'

'Even when you're sitting with Edgar?' I asked lightly, teasingly.

'Of course I will – it's only boys who can't multi-task.'

Friday December 13th

7.01 a.m.
Woke up feeling all shivery. Ha! Friday 13th – what did I expect?

'Nerves,' I said to myself, a bit surprised. I felt hot too and every bone in my body ached. Those nerves really have kicked in, I thought. Still never suspecting anything until I threw up in the bathroom. That's when horror seized hold of me. And when I knew the forty-eight-hour tummy bug that had been rampaging round my school – and which I'd hoped would settle on Beachy Head – had swerved right past him and made instead – for me.

Of all the days to be ill! This is, without doubt, the worst ever ...

And I couldn't let my parents know how

rotten I was feeling either as, yes, they would be quite sympathetic. My mum is always really nice when you're suffering. But then she'd say while concernedly mopping my brow, 'Oh now, Louis, you're far too ill to go to school (hurrah) or travel to London tonight to appear on *Kids with Attitude*.'

And nothing on earth would make me miss that. Not even if I had three diseases. So I suppose I'm lucky really that I've just got the one. And it's not a disease or anything. No, I've just got a stomach which explodes every so often – like NOW.

7.15 a.m.
Back again. And I must have got rid of most of my sick now. I mean, I've spewed out tons of the frothing stuff. I've also sprayed the bathroom with all the smellies I could find so Mum and Dad don't suspect anything. Then I bunged a whole load of smellies on me in case I'm a bit whiffy too.

9.00 a.m.
I probably overdid that, as a couple of boys at school have just held their noses as I wafted past them.

11.00 a.m.

The second it was break time I tore into the loo. Still more sick gushed out of me. Also, my head was throbbing like a motorcycle and all I really wanted was to curl up in a corner and sleep. But I mustn't be sent home ill. I can do this.

1.50 p.m.

People from my class have just been asking me about the *Kids with Attitude* Final tonight. Stuff like:

'What's the prize if you win – not that you will win?'

'What will you do if you lose to that parrot again?'

'Are you going to be funny this time?'

'Hey, I'll have you all laughing like crazy tonight,' I said, before adding under my breath, 'if I live that long.' Now, even when I sit down I feel as if I'm about to pass out.

1.55 p.m.

Just had a horrible thought. What if, when I'm in the car with Dad on the way to *Kids with Attitude*, I need to explode some more of the yukky stuff? What will I do? Somehow hold it in all the way to London. But what if I can't? Well, if Dad suspects I'm not well, he'll insist they

151

turn the car round and bundle me off to bed.

I need help.

1.56 p.m.
Maddy.

3.00 p.m.
Maddy's phone was switched off so I sent her all these texts telling her to call me urgently, and she's finally just rung me now. I quickly explained to her about my perilous state of health.

'So how do you feel now?' she asked.

'Worse every second.'

'Oh no.'

'But don't worry, when I get out on that stage I'll knock 'em dead.'

'Doctor Greasepaint.'

'What?'

'However ill people feel, when they're up on the stage performing, all their aches and pains just fall away.'

'That's good to know.' Then I told Maddy my worry about the car journey.

'Just tell your dad you're car-sick.'

'Yeah. Only I've never been car-sick before.'

'Say you've got bad nerves then,' she said.

'Mmm,' I said doubtfully. 'Or ... or ...' I

hesitated.

'Please don't say,' cried Maddy, 'you're asking me to drop Edgar and go with you instead?'

'No, of course not,' I said at once. 'Well, maybe a bit.'

'Oh, Louis …'

'I just thought when I felt another explosion coming on I could cough twice – and that would be like our secret ringtone for you to say you feel ill. Then you'll exit the car accompanied by me. I throw up and we get back in the car with Dad none the wiser.'

'It sounds a lovely way to spend an evening!'

'It's only the first part.'

'But I can't let Edgar down, can I?'

I let Maddy's question just hang in the air. Then finally I said, 'Don't worry, I'll work on being car-sick.'

Two minutes later Maddy called me back. 'What time do you leave for London?'

3.50 p.m.

Maddy will be round any second. And the car taking us to the studio is due in about ten minutes. It's all about to happen.

Mum and Elliot have both wished me luck. But the atmosphere is still not good, especially with Dad. He's polite enough but very distant.

Still, on the bright side, I haven't thrown up for hours. And if I can win tonight, well, that trumps everything, doesn't it?

Chapter Seventeen
You're the Winner

Thursday December 12th

4.35 p.m.

We were in the car – Dad chatting to the driver in the front, Maddy and me in the back and probably about halfway to the studio, when several shudders ran through me at once. Horrible, slimy sick was waiting to explode from my mouth once more. I didn't even trust myself to speak. I just coughed twice. Maddy instantly recognized our signal and she called out, 'Excuse me, but I feel a little nauseous.'

Dad turned round and smiled reassuringly at Maddy. 'You're probably just a bit car-sick.

155

Don't worry, it happens to us all.'

The driver popped his head round too. 'Always carry these with me – barley sugars. It'll settle your stomach, all right.'

Maddy took one and sucked it thoughtfully, while I writhed in silent agony, feeling worse and worse.

Finally I hissed, 'Maddy, how does you sitting there sucking barley sugars help me? It's no good saying you feel *a little nauseous*. You've got to be really dramatic – and quick.'

'All right, calm down, I just haven't got finally into the part yet,' Maddy hissed back. 'I need to warm up, you know – even athletes before a race have to ...'

'Maddy, just do something and fast,' I groaned.

'Everything all right in the back?' asked Dad.

That's when Maddy let out a scream, which even made me jump. Then she grabbed hold of the car handle and shrieked, 'I'm going to be extremely sick this very instant! Stop the car!'

The driver didn't need telling twice. 'There's a sort of wood over there,' he said, pointing.

'I'll go with you,' I managed to splutter.

'So will I,' began Dad.

'No, Louis will be fine,' said Maddy firmly.

We tore out of the car, and as soon as we were out of sight I really let myself go.

'Sorry,' I said to Maddy, who was hovering very near to the area I'd just decorated.

'No, better out than in,' said Maddy, 'as my granny always says ... you might want to wipe your mouth now.'

'Oh, yeah, sorry.' And while I was cleaning my face with my hankie I added, 'That was a top scream, by the way.'

'Oh, thanks ... I was rather pleased with it. I knew once I got into my role ...'

'You were terrific and totally believable.'

Maddy smiled modestly then asked, 'So how do you feel now?'

'Honestly?' I said. 'Pretty awful.'

'I so wish I could get rid of this bug for you.' And right then I could feel her keenness to help me, like the warmth of a fire. It wasn't just because she was my agent either. She liked me. I was sure of it. And I so liked her. That's why I burst out, 'I know this is totally the wrong moment, but would you ever reconsider and go on a second date with me?'

Maddy looked at me. 'There's still a bit of sick in your hair ... and it looks like a bit on your shoes.'

'I'm disgusting,' I said, wiping the shoe with my hankie while vigorously rubbing my hair with my other hand.

Then Maddy said, 'We'd better go back,' so totally ignoring my question.

4.55 p.m.
Just a quick message from the Green Room (I love saying that but it's really only a waiting room). All twelve of us finalists are here, with our families circling round, whispering words of encouragement, as if we were prize-fighters about to step into the ring.

I grinned at Ben, the boy who does the act with Benny the parrot. (Benny is apparently resting off stage.) But otherwise the contestants don't even look – let alone talk – to each other. We're each waiting inside our own little bubble.

5.00 p.m.
Evie, the researcher, has bounced in, as enthusiastic and smiley as ever, her hair still orange. Standing beside her was a young guy in an expensive grey suit with gloomy hangdog eyes, like a world-weary St Bernard dog. She introduced him as Ned, the producer.

'First of all,' she said, 'I want you to give yourselves a little pat on the back for getting this far.' She waited but no one moved. That was way too uncool. We weren't three years old. 'Thanks so much for doing that,' she said brightly and wholly inaccurately. 'Now I shall ask your family and friends to go and make themselves comfortable in the studio and act as our very enthusiastic audience.'

So that left just us with Evie and Ned.

Evie beamed round at us again. 'Well, you don't need me to tell you what a wonderful chance this is for you all. We want you to live this show tonight, breathe it, *own* it.'

'And remember, put everything you've got into it,' chipped in Ned. That was the only thing he said to us.

'To get us into the vibe,' Evie added, 'I want you all to shout out, "I'm a winner," right now.'

We did – but not loud enough. It took four more attempts before Evie was satisfied.

'Now that was wonderful,' she grinned. 'Well done, everyone. Have a fabulous show. I will be back with the running order for the rehearsal very soon.'

After she and Ned left, I grinned round at some of the other contestants, but we were all too tense and worked up to talk much. A few people were messing about on their phones, one girl was doing deep breathing exercises, while another seemed to be taking a photograph of one of her shoes.

And then I let out a truly massive burp. I

suppose it broke the tension. Everyone laughed anyway. 'Sorry about my very rude stomach,' I said.

'It's just nerves,' said a cheerful-looking girl in a wheelchair.

I so wish it was.

5.52 p.m.
The rehearsal's just finished. We were on the very stage we'd be performing on tonight, but with only the first couple of rows full with 'our supporters', as Evie called them. I was second to last on. (Evie decided the rehearsal order by pulling our names out of a hat.) So, how did it go? Better than I'd ever dreamed possible. I was pretty good, but Felix was even better. No, honestly, he was sensational.

He told me one joke – and can you believe I never quite know what he's going to say? – which the audience loved. Here it is:

A man is driving along with three penguins in the back of the car. Then a policeman stops him and says, 'You should take them to the zoo.'

He says he will.

But the next day the policeman also stops the car again and there are those three penguins again. Only this time one of them is wearing sunglasses. 'I thought I told you to take those penguins to the zoo,' said the policeman.

'So I did,' says the man. 'And today I'm taking them to the seaside.'

I'm definitely keeping that in my act – or rather Felix is.

Afterwards Dad shook me by the hand. 'That was so original,' he said.

Then Maddy said to me, 'It's a tough gig, as some of the singers were excellent and that magician ...'

'Scarily brilliant,' I agreed.

Then Maddy whispered in my ear, 'But you're the winner.'

I looked at her.

'I'm not just saying it because I'm your agent. It's what I really believe. How do you feel?' she added softly.

'I've never felt mouldier, but when I was out there I forgot how rotten—'

'I told you – Dr Greasepaint,' she interrupted. 'He'll save you next time as well.'

6.10 p.m.
The Green Room again.

We're all back here. A couple of kids seem to be glued to their gushy parents. But the rest of

161

us contestants have been jostling round each other, chatting and laughing and showing each other pictures of ourselves taken twenty seconds ago on our iPhones.

I chatted the longest to Ben. He's dead worried about Benny. You see, Ben played his mouth organ as usual, but for the first time ever Benny had refused to sing a note. All through their act he just sat on his perch ruffling his feathers.

'Perhaps he's holding out for more seed,' I said.

'I'd even taught him to do a little dance,' said Ben. 'That was our extra surprise.'

But instead the surprise was Benny didn't do anything at all. I patted Ben on the back. 'He'll be fine when the theatre is buzzing with people. Benny demands a full house.'

A little mean part of me wished Benny would remain on strike (well, he did beat me last time). But like Maddy, I had a feeling I could win this competition fair and square.

There was one person I was worried about though. And she was the very last contestant I spoke to – Poppy. She'd whizzed on stage in her wheelchair. But she had this tray over the chair and then proceeded to do not one, not two, but three magic tricks at once. It was incredibly fast and totally brilliant.

She suddenly steamed towards me.

'I'm not talking to you,' I said. 'You're way too good!'

'What are you talking about?' she cried. 'You and Felix were amazing.'

'But what about you doing all those tricks at once – and I loved the way you kept swooping about on the stage.'

'I can go fast, can't I?' she said proudly.

She was a pretty, dark-haired girl with the most piercing blue eyes I'd ever seen. 'So where did you learn all those tricks?' I asked. 'Did you go on some sort of course?'

'No, it's all thanks to him.' She nodded at an elderly guy in a green suit with a bright red handkerchief gushing out of his top pocket. He was sporting a black fedora hat, and was talking very animatedly to Evie. 'Grandad used to be in show business,' she said, and just by glancing at him I could believe that, 'but poor Grandad never got the breaks he deserved. And he says so much of success is down to luck. Anyway, after Mum died he turned all his attention to me. He's taught me everything I know.'

Poppy's grandad suddenly spotted us and must have somehow guessed we were talking about him as he bowed lavishly. He was about to come over too when Evie announced it was time for our supporters to return to the theatre.

'Break a leg,' said Dad. 'Do people still say that?'

'I've never heard them. And it sounds a bit weird, but thanks.'

'Just be as good as you were in rehearsal,' said Dad. Then he smiled at me for the first time in about three days. 'And all the best, son.'

Maddy just whispered to me again those three magic words, 'You're the winner.'

Now six of the contestants – including Poppy and Ben – have left for make-up. And everyone left has gone a bit quiet again.

So how am I feeling? I'd better not tell you. You'd only worry. And believe me, I'm worried enough for both of us. But as Maddy said I'll be totally fine once I hit that stage again.

6.25 p.m.
The make-up lady had to work on me twice. Once when it was my turn. But then she popped up again, putting more powder on my face because it was still glistening with sweat. 'You're not nervous, are you, darlin'?' she asked.

I could see why she'd think that as sweat seemed to be oozing from my every pore. But I knew what was really causing it. My hideous bug, reminding me it's still lurking there.

6.35 p.m.

Evie's been giving us more details about the show. 'As you're all winners the audience won't have trumpets this time.' (In the earlier rounds kids could blow little trumpets if they didn't like your act.) But when your three minutes are up you will hear a loud trumpet call – and that means you must finish your act at once. If you don't I will come on stage and ask you to leave. I don't want to do that and I'm sure you'd rather avoid the humiliation too. Now I have some very exciting news for you – Mickey Boyd is going to introduce the show.'

I'd vaguely heard of him. He'd been in a boy band yonks ago, then hosted a game show on television. And now he was doing something similar on this channel (not that I'd ever really watched it).

'Now Mickey's dropping by to say hello,' said Evie, and she couldn't have sounded more excited.

A surprisingly short guy in a white T-shirt, black jacket and jeans bounded in, oozing confidence from every pore and yelled, 'Weyheyhey' – this was his catchphrase in the Stone Age – 'stars of tomorrow. Meet a star for all time.' Evie threw back her head and laughed, as if he'd just made the funniest joke in the world. 'I can appreciate what a thrill it must be meeting me,' he added, and he and Evie laughed again. He was sort of joking and sort of wasn't. 'But don't be over-awed or nervous when you're on stage with me. I will say a few brief words and then it's over to you. Just be mega-tastic, OK?'

'Super thanks for that,' cooed Evie. 'And I know our contestants would appreciate any words of wisdom you have for them.'

'All right,' said Mickey Boyd, 'my advice to all of you is this – if you need to nip out for a wee-wee, now's the time. Weyheyhey.'

Evie laughed so hard at this I wouldn't have been very surprised if she'd had to nip out herself.

And then our audience with this legend in his own head was over.

'So good of Mickey to come and talk to you all before the show, wasn't it?' said Evie.

No one answered. I muttered to Poppy, 'Weyhey, poseur.'

6.42 p.m.
I'd just paid another visit to the loo (I'll spare you the gory details) when I spotted Poppy bombing along in the corridor in her wheelchair. She had her hat and scarf on as well, which I thought

was a bit strange. Then as she whirled past me she called out, 'Bye, Louis, hope you win.'

'Where are you going?' I called.

She stopped. 'Home,' she said.

I steamed over to her. 'What are you talking about? You aced it ...'

'Just a fluke,' she interrupted. 'You see, I've got very big thumbs.'

'Your whole career is over then. Having big thumbs is just catastrophic.' I bent down and I made a big point of studying them. 'I'm sure I saw bigger thumbs in a horror film once. No, they look fine. Honestly.'

She shook her head. 'Also, I was shaking before I went out last time.'

'We all were. But when you got on the stage you gave it everything you've got.'

'I can't do it again, though. I know I can't. I'll get Grandad to film me doing tricks and put them up on YouTube. That will be as good. Well, nearly. I really do hope you win.' Then she started wheeling herself away again.

If she wanted to leave so much, should I just let her go? After all, she was my biggest competitor! I was dead tempted to wave her off, I can tell you. But in the end I knew I just couldn't.

'If you go home now,' I called after her, 'I'll

never talk to you again. You might think that's another good reason for leaving. But you'll also never forgive yourself for squandering this massive chance, which you might never get again because of some rubbish about giant thumbs and peaking too soon. Anyway, I know the real reason you're leaving? Want to hear what it is?'

'Go on, then.' Poppy had stopped and her eyes had grown even larger as she looked up at me.

'You're just suffering from a massive attack of nerves. And that's fantastic.'

'Why is it?'

I walked towards her. 'Because it means you're dead keen to be good. In fact, if you didn't have nerves that's when you should be worried. So you've got absolutely no worries at all. Want to know something else? Everyone here is dead nervous, including me. Especially me.'

'Actually, you do look a bit sweaty.'

'Thanks for sharing that.' And at that moment I swayed back from her, feeling very, very groggy suddenly.

'Louis, are you all right?'

'Oh yeah, I just got a proper look at your thumbs. They are incredible. In fact, they should have their own television series.'

Poppy was still laughing when Evie called

down the corridor. 'I'm about to pull the names out of the bag for the last time – the most important time – so back to the Green Room everyone.'

I looked down at Poppy. 'Decision time.'

After just a beat of silence she said softly, 'You know, I might just stay after all.'

'And if you win tonight – which you probably will – I'll so wish I'd let you go home.'

6.50 p.m.
Ben and Benny the parrot are on first. Ben doesn't look pleased about that. I pat him on the back. Then I hear who's second. Me. Not as bad as going on first, but close.

7.04 p.m.
I'm waiting in the wings now and furious. Mickey Boyd is introducing the show by plugging his own. He's droning on and on about himself. Centuries pass by before he finally even mentions Ben and Benny.

7.07 p.m.
Ben comes on at last valiantly playing his mouth organ and desperately trying to lure the parrot into doing something, anything. And suddenly Benny lets out the most bloodthirsty scream

169

before soaring off the stage. Ben stands there for a few moments, frozen with shocked horror and unsure what to do next. A few of the audience even boo him, which I think was pretty mean. Then he exits too.

But will he and Benny return?

I can hear a few squawks offstage from the great parrot, but that's all.

7.10 p.m.
I really don't think either Ben or Benny are coming back, which means I could be on any second.

7.11 p.m.
Evie is telling me to get ready. *This is it.* I am electrified with excitement until my stomach gives a truly thundering lurch. I know that's a warning. It's about to explode any second.

In fact, now.

But it can't, because this is my big chance – and now Evie is signalling me to go on stage …

Chapter Eighteen

The Great Yukky Experience

9.45 p.m.

Dear Diary, I'd give anything to make tonight disappear.

If I could turn back time – just for a few hours – what an incredibly brilliant superpower that would be. For then I could blot out ...

But I can't and, live on TV tonight I have ...

I have so let myself down.

The gruesomeness started when I staggered onto the stage, feeling sicker every second. In rehearsal, we'd practised where we had to stand, which was right next to Mickey Boyd.

The spotlight flared on both of us.

I had to tell Mickey Boyd I needed to leave this very second and then speed to the nearest loo. Once I'd extinguished all the vile stuff and cleaned myself up, I'd probably be allowed back on stage. I could even make some jokes about it. All was not lost – provided I acted *now*.

The trouble was, Mickey Boyd wasn't even looking at me. Instead, he'd spotted someone in the audience – a very pretty woman in the second row. He was going 'Weyheyhey' to her and she was really playing up to him.

I took some deep breaths. Didn't help. Then I saw Evie getting twitchy in the wings and tapping her watch. Mickey Boyd didn't notice Evie either. All his attention was still beamed on the nice-looking lady in the second row.

But I couldn't wait another second. So I swallowed hard and shouted, 'Going to have to stop you there, Mickey.' He whirled round – and at the very same moment spotted Evie signalling wildly to him in the wings. A furious gleam came into his eyes as he thought Evie and I were trying to speed him up – no one is allowed to do that to a legend like him.

So, flashing his dazzling, white teeth, Mickey yelled, 'I think our young friend is getting impatient. Or maybe,' he smiled at the woman in the second row, 'he just wants to be introduced. Well, who can blame him?' Then he stretched out his hand and yanked me towards him. It was the sudden movement that did it. Took me completely by surprise. That's why before I knew what was happening I'd thrown up all over Mickey Boyd.

I couldn't help it. I couldn't stop it.

My mouth was suddenly ablaze with vomit, which exploded out of my mouth so fast that within seconds I'd totally covered Mickey Boyd in chopped carrots. And not only his face dripped with the stuff – you could see it glistening and gleaming all down his jacket too.

I was mortified. I was horrified. And if Mickey Boyd had turned round and punched me I really wouldn't have blamed him.

Instead, he just went on standing there with vile-looking yellow stuff still dribbling down his chin. But incredibly his face remained, even now, frozen into a big wide Mickey Boyd smile.

Meanwhile the audience didn't laugh or shout or anything. There was just this deep pool of shocked silence, the most deafening you've ever heard.

I had to at least say something, try and apologize. So I opened my mouth, but no words actually came out. I just spluttered like water on a hot stove, until a small army of people, led by Ned and Evie, surged onto the stage. Totally ignoring me they devoted all their attention to pacifying and escorting away a dripping – but still grinning – Mickey Boyd.

As Mickey left, some of the audience clapped him. There were even a few cheers. Meanwhile, a guy with a crew-cut and with a very angry-looking boil on his neck lumbered on stage and half dragged me, now quivering with shame, away too. I guessed he was a security man, but I never got a chance to discuss his profession with him. He was a man of few words, two of them which were, 'In there' when we reached the loo.

But I'd used up my current quota of sick. So I just cleaned myself up and then heard a girl trilling away. The show was going on again. That cheered me up greatly, even made me wonder if I could go back on.

I began to picture the scene. I'd return doing my act with Felix and make the audience fall about laughing. Then as I finished the whole room would be on their feet cheering wildly for this boy who'd entertained everyone so brilliantly despite being very, very ill.

What actually happened was the man with the angry boil led me down some corridors. At first I thought I was returning to the dressing room to have some more make-up daubed onto me. But instead I was taken to the back of the studios, where a door clanged open.

He pointed, 'Wait outside there.'

'Am I going home?' I asked.

He nodded and was gone. I stood there for a few seconds under the dark sky. Then a car whirled up. The driver was the same one who'd driven us here. He frowned heavily at me as I plonked down in the back.

And we sat there in silence until Dad and Maddy half ran towards the car, with their heads down, as if they were caught up in my shame.

Dad opened the front car door and shouted, 'I hear from Maddy you've got a nasty stomach bug. Why on earth didn't you tell me before?'

'Because I thought you'd stop me coming here tonight,' I muttered wearily. 'And now I so wished you had.'

Dad let out a huge sigh. 'I don't trust myself to say anything else to you right now.'

The driver, not to be left out, released a huge sigh too, and then said snappily, 'If you or your friend want to be sick, then shout, all right? I've just had this car cleaned.' He didn't offer us any more barley sugars either.

I whispered to Maddy, 'I've really messed up

175

this time, haven't I?'

She murmured, 'Everyone throws up at some time. Everyone.'

'Not live on TV they don't.'

Maddy couldn't answer that one. So instead, she just squeezed my hand really tightly.

I forced a smile. 'I bet you're dead sorry you dumped me now.'

When I got home I had another mini-explosion of chucking up. Then I fell backwards onto my bed and that's where I am now.

Unsurprisingly, I don't seem to be in an especially great mood (understatement!). Hey, I can't even think of a joke. So best if I just sign off.

Thanks for your company and sorry to have let you down tonight.

THE END.

PROBABLY.

Louis the Sick

Chapter Nineteen

Take Over

Saturday December 14th

12.30 p.m.

Hi, I'm Felix. I expect you've heard of me. The good news is that I'm taking over this diary. Where's Louis? Well, if you're at all interested, he's lying in bed still feeling incredibly groggy. But that's not what's really bugging him.

His big dream was always to be a comedian. Well, after last night I'd say he needs to find another dream, wouldn't you? How about training wasps. I'm sure there are some vacancies there. Ha ha.

To be honest, I never thought Louis was that

funny. Well, not compared to me. I'm the real star of the act, because I know far better jokes like:

Why was the man running in his bedroom?
He wanted to catch up with his sleep.

We're going to have a great time together.

12.40 p.m.
Oh yeah, just in case you were wondering what happened on *Kids with Attitude*. Mickey Boyd returned to the stage in new clothes! He got a standing ovation which he lapped up and the show went on as normal. The winner, by the way, was Poppy. Her prize, of course, her own half-hour Christmas show which she records next week. And if Louis had to lose to anyone I know he would have liked it to be her. So that's the one bit of good news.

As for Louis himself – he is acting like a total recluse, not even answering any of his Facebook messages. Still, can you blame him?

Now here's a seasonal joke:

What do you get when you cross a snowman with a vampire?
Frostbite.

Louis never told you a joke as funny as that, did he?

Sunday December 15th

4.50 p.m.
In case you were worried – which you weren't – Louis is now out of bed and slurping soup. Yeah, he's finally stopped being sick.

6.00 p.m.
'That's a moment of your life you'll want to forget.'

It took a moment for Louis to realize his mum was talking about his spot of forgery, not his mega–embarrassing appearance on telly. She went on, 'We all make mistakes, but the important thing is to learn from them.' She added, 'As for what happened to you on Friday when you appeared on television – it seems huge now, but just ask yourself how this will seem in five years' time – hope that's helped you put it in perspective.'

It hadn't.

And Louis is still grounded until the New Year.

And he's got to go back to school tomorrow. Good luck with that one.

How about a school joke?

Why was the maths book sad?
Because it had too many problems.

Monday December 16th

4.10 p.m.
Louis walked to school with his head partly hidden under a Father Christmas hat.

And then it started.

Some boys thought they were being hilarious, by jumping away from Louis as if they were afraid he was going to be sick on them. Others asked him stuff like:

'Did you do it deliberately?'

And, 'Which celebrity will you get next?'

Another boy told him how he'd watched someone be sick on their friend's head on a rollercoaster – but what Louis did was ten times more disgusting. I think he meant it as a compliment.

But every girl only said one word when they saw Louis. 'Gross.'

By the afternoon Louis had even acquired a new nickname. He'd hate you to know what it is, so of course I'll tell you – it's *Vomit Boy*. Wherever he goes that name now follows him.

I'd so hate to be called that, wouldn't you?

Anyway, what happened to the wasp that got run over?

It was taken to waspital.

Tuesday December 17th

Maddy's just called Louis to tell him that the video of him spewing up over Mickey Boyd has gone viral.

'It's a YouTube sensation,' she cried.

'And that's good because ...?' he asked very bitterly.

Her voice fell away. 'Well, it means lots of people are seeing you.'

'The most hideous version of me ever ... but still, who knows, maybe my puke will get its own show?'

'Oh, Louis, don't be like that ... you're famous, sort of.'

'But I don't want to be just known as that disgusting boy who threw up over Mickey—'

'Oh yes,' interrupted Maddy, 'Mickey Boyd is all over the place, laughing it off. And he's going to be on the next series of *Celebrity Masterchef*. Mum says he hasn't been on terrestrial telly for years, so he's benefited from—'

'I'm really happy for him,' said Louis. 'I'm

really happy for everyone except me.'

'I'm only trying to help.'

'I wouldn't bother.'

'I won't then … and I don't know why you've got the mega-hump with me,' she added in a small voice. She rang off before he could reply.

Louis knows she is only trying to help.

But the very last thing he wants are people – and especially Maddy – pitying him.

He has some pride left. Somewhere. But mainly he is just bursting with shame.

Joke time.

What do you call a sleeping bull?

A bulldozer.

I bet you're not missing Louis at all, are you?

Chapter Twenty
On the Run

Wednesday December 18th

5.10 p.m.

Yo, Louis the Laugh is back.

Well, Felix was getting way too big-headed.

And I've got a bit of an exclusive for you. I've just made a massive decision. But first, I didn't think I could be any more fed up after another day of 'Vomit Boy' and yet another mind-blowingly, boring detention. But on the way home a girl about sixteen sped up to me. I'd never seen her before but she looked dead excited.

'Wow! It's really you, isn't it?'

'It was, the last time I checked,' I grinned.

She wanted a selfie. I agreed at once. I was even a bit flattered until she added, 'And you've got to look as if you're throwing up.'

'Oh, have I?' I said highly unenthusiastically.

'Of course, there's no point in the picture otherwise,' she said.

So I valiantly impersonated someone chucking up. But then I told her. 'Actually, I went on *Kids with Attitude* to tell jokes. It was a great act as well. Here's a quick sample: Why did the tomato blush? *Because it saw the salad dressing.* Do you like that one?'

She didn't answer because she wasn't even listening. She was on her mobile. 'Yeah, you know that really gross boy on YouTube, well, I told you he lived near me and I've just seen him ...'

I stared at her sadly. 'My dream was to *tell* jokes, not *be* a joke.'

But of course she didn't hear that either.

Trudging home, I thought, I can't go on leading the life of an international laughing-stock. It's time for me to fight back. So that's what I'm going to do – by running away.

Early tomorrow I will escape to my grandparents.

Not my dad's mum and dad, who live nearby, but my mum's lot who reside in a small village in deepest Suffolk.

You can't ever get a decent mobile phone signal there. And if you ever want to talk to anyone you have to resort to a very ancient invention called a landline. Plus Nan and Grandad don't even have a television, let alone a computer. They're too busy collecting frogspawn and waiting for the steam train. I used to hate staying there. I said it was like time-travelling back to the 1950s, but now it seems the perfect hideaway.

My grandparents don't actually know I'm visiting them yet. But I figured if I roll up at their cottage – and just before Christmas as well – they're hardly going to turn me away, are they? I'd like to stay with them for at least a year. But I won't tell them that on my first night. I'll build up to that.

I've had some Christmas money early, so that will cover my train fare, provided I leave after half past nine. So here's my plan. I'll act as if I'm taking off for school as usual, but instead I'll slip off to the railway station. And by this time tomorrow I'll be happily residing in the place time forgot.

There I'll give Mum and Dad a friendly call, probably just before they go off and see Elliot in *Oliver*. I'll also gently remind them they've still got time to post off my Christmas presents.

I really have thought of everything.

7.05 p.m.
Of all people, Edgar has just turned up at my house.

Elliot opened the door, and then gazed at Edgar in his tweed blazer with elbow patches.

'Is he for real?' he whispered to me.

'Unfortunately yes,' I hissed back.

Everyone was in the sitting room so I took Edgar into the kitchen. 'This is an unexpected …' I began. 'Well, it's unexpected anyway.'

'Hold onto your hat,' cried Edgar. 'But I have asked Maddy to put on her dancing shoes.'

'What!'

'There's a party at the local home for elderly citizens to mark the start of the festive season. I assist there, so I shall be joining in the celebrations. There will also be some light refreshments, I'm not sure exactly what. But there may be crisps.'

'Wow.'

'And Maddy has agreed to accompany me.' Suddenly Edgar was studying me very closely.

'OK, that's fine,' I said.

'Really?' He sounded almost disappointed.

'Yeah, though I just can't imagine you dancing.' And I began to laugh.

'My preferred choice of music for a party would be the sound of a harpsichord,' said Edgar.

'Sorry, are we in the seventeenth century?'

'But I shall adapt myself to my surroundings,' said Edgar, 'as I think this would be a perfect environment at which to ask Maddy out.' I stopped laughing. He went on, 'And I am certain, within an acceptable margin of error, that this time she will say yes.'

For a moment I just stood there as my heart leaped about before finally smashing into my front teeth.

I'd hoped, wished that somehow Maddy and me would get back together ...

But enough of that, I quickly told myself. I was hardly even speaking to Maddy these days. And as I'm fleeing to the country and probably wouldn't see her again for at least a year ... well, Maddy deserved a boyfriend. And why not Edgar? Lots of reasons, actually.

But Edgar was a big success now. Despite — or maybe because of his eccentricity – he'd been invited back on to local telly to read some more poems on New Year's Eve.

Yes, why not Edgar?

So I just said, 'Thanks for letting me know.'

Edgar didn't speak for a moment (highly unusual) and went on watching me anxiously.

187

'No, I'm really OK about it, honestly,' I insisted.

'Thank you,' he said. 'I wanted to do the honourable thing and tell you.'

'Which you've just done.' Then I stared very pointedly at the door.

But instead he asked, 'Got any plans for Christmas?'

'I'm going away.'

'Soon?' asked Edgar.

'Very soon,' I said firmly.

Edgar turned to leave. 'You know you've gone viral.'

'Not a bit interested,' I said shortly.

'Well, then, I have some good news for you. The Internet is just a fad.'

'Says who?'

'Me,' said Edgar. 'People are soon going to get very tired of living their lives through a screen. I give it two more years at the most.' Then he bowed low. 'Good evening.'

7.40 p.m.

That was a close one. I was packing away a few things for my extended stay in Suffolk when Mum came nosing in. I only just hid my schoolbag away in time.

'What have I done now?' I asked.

'For once, nothing,' said Mum. She sat down

on my bed. 'We just wondered how you were feeling?'

'Mum, I'm a boy, so I never talk about feelings with anyone. It's the law.'

'A very silly law too,' said Mum at once. 'I know this hasn't been an easy week for you – and you've seemed far away from everyone and hardly saying anything. In fact, talking to you has been like talking to an old sock.'

'Talk to many old socks, do you, Mum?'

Mum grinned. 'Now there's the old Louis we know and love.'

'Glad someone does,' I muttered. 'No, Mum, I'm fine, honestly.'

'OK,' said Mum. 'I don't want to press you, but if ever you want to talk about anything ...'

'I know where you live.' Then as I wouldn't be seeing Mum for a while I said suddenly. 'Mum, have a good ...' I was going to say 'Christmas', but I hastily changed it to 'life'.

Mum looked a bit surprised, but then she must have thought I was trying to be funny as she just smiled and added, 'By the way, your dad's got some exciting news. But I'll let him tell you about that.'

8.10 p.m.
Dad's exciting news is that he's got a meeting

189

with some business colleagues tomorrow at nine o'clock. 'In London, is it?' I asked.

'Er yes, that's right,' said Dad. 'Nothing is promised but it could be very useful.'

'I'm happy for you, Dad,' I said.

Things were better between Dad and me now, but nowhere near as close as they had been before. This was partly of course because I was in detention every night, so not coming home much earlier than Mum or Elliot. But it wasn't only that. So I said, 'All the very best for tomorrow, Dad.'

I sort of meant it too. He deserved another job.

Thursday December 19th

8.45 a.m.
Left home with a schoolbag containing not a single thing for school, but everything I'm taking to Suffolk. My time on the run has begun.

8.55 a.m.
I'd just arrived at the station when this youngish guy pointed at me, then pretended to be scared. 'Hey, don't throw up on me.'

I nearly died with not laughing.

I'm fleeing not a moment too soon.

190

11.30 a.m.
A great deal has happened.

I'd just joined the queue for tickets when a voice behind me said, 'Gotcha.'

I whirled round.

'I so knew you were going to do this.'

Chapter Twenty-One
Urgent Message

11.30 a.m. (cont'd)

I was stunned. 'What are you doing here?'

'I knew it,' said Maddy again, positively bursting with pride. 'Then Edgar just confirmed my suspicions.'

'Edgar! What's he got to do with this?'

'Oh, I sent him round to you.'

'Why would you do something as mean as that?'

'Well, you were hardly talking to me.'

'I was hardly talking to anyone. I just wanted to be alone with my shame. That's hardly surprising, is it?'

Maddy sighed. 'Sometimes, Louis, you act

just like a big baby.'

'Thanks for that.'

'But Edgar thought he could find out your plans. So he told you all that stuff about taking me dancing …'

'That's not true, then?'

'Oh yes,' she said casually.

I wondered if him asking Maddy out was true too.

'But he was hoping to get a reaction from you, and when he didn't he knew things were bad. He waited until you were relaxed before he asked you the really important question – top detectives do that, you know – about your plans for Christmas. When you said you were going away very soon, we both knew you were about to run away. So we watched your house this morning and then I followed you here. Where are you off to, then?'

'To my grandparents, the ones who live in Suffolk.'

'And how long are you staying there?'

'Until people forget or I die of old age.'

That's when Maddy started to laugh. Normally that's the best sound in the world, but on the extremely rare occasion when you're trying to be serious, trust me, it's not.

So I said, all huffily, 'I'm so glad I've amused

you. And thanks for seeing me off, but you needn't have bothered. I hope you and Edgar have fun dancing and whatever else you're planning to do together. But my new life is calling me. I'll send you a smoke signal when I'm settled – and have a top Christmas.'

I'd actually turned away from her when Maddy tapped me on the shoulder. I slowly turned round again, and then Maddy let out a sigh that was more like a hiss. 'Do you really think I'm here just to wave you goodbye as I sob into my hankie?' Before I could reply she added, 'And if you buy a ticket I'll shove it up your backside.'

The woman in front of me let out a gasp. I nearly gasped too. I'd never seen Maddy so worked up before. And it was a school day, so she'd bunked off school to come and find me, something she wouldn't have done lightly.

'Now, come on,' she said, 'you're not going anywhere today, as I've got things to tell you.'

'What?' I asked at once.

Maddy walked away. 'Come and find out.' And I found myself following her.

'We can't talk here,' she said. 'Too conspicuous.' So we went round to the back of the station where people were already queuing for taxis.

'All I can say,' I said, 'is that this had better

be good.'

'First of all, Louis, as your agent, I have to tell you that no one can take your destiny away from you.'

'You got me out of the queue to tell me that.'

'No,' replied Maddy. 'I've also got some news for you. But first, I have never been ashamed of you before. Not ever, but today I am. Just sloping off without a word to me, your agent—'

'What's the news?' I interrupted.

She stared at me for a moment, and then in a voice shaking with emotion, 'Poppy wants you to ring her urgently.'

'Poppy!' I repeated.

'Yeah, the girl who won ...'

'I know who she is ...'

'She's been trying to contact you for days. Left all these messages on your Facebook page.'

'I haven't been answering anyone.'

'Then finally she got in touch with me late last night in a right state. I tried calling you but your phone was switched off, as usual.'

'Why's she so desperate to talk to me?'

'Call her and find out,' said Maddy.

'I haven't got her number.'

'But I have,' said Maddy, her voice shaking with excitement again. 'And she's in the studio all day.'

That last sentence hit me smack in the heart. Of course, Poppy's in a television studio – working on the special half-hour winner's show. For a moment I so ached for that to be me. Then Maddy handed me the phone. 'It's ringing, but Poppy might be in a bad mood with you.'

She was.

'I've been bombarding you with messages for about eight centuries and you've ignored every one of them,' she said.

'Look, it's nothing personal. It's just since I embarrassed myself, well, I've become a total joke everywhere. Do you know what I'm known as at school now? *Vomit Boy*.'

I waited for her to show sympathy for the tragic turn my life had taken. Instead, she snapped. 'Oh, poor you, poor, poor you, Louis. You've been called "Vomit Boy", for what, five days, six days? And people will get bored of it soon. By the New Year it'll be practically forgotten. You'll see. But do you know what I'm called every day of my life? The Wheelchair Girl. People look at me and that's the first thing – the *only* thing – they can see.'

'Yeah, OK, and that's dead annoying,' I conceded. 'But I'm not feeling sorry for you because you've won.'

'And have you read what people are saying on

Twitter about that?

'No, what?'

'They said the only reason I won was because I'm in a wheelchair. It was all just a huge sympathy vote.'

'That's total rubbish.'

'Thanks.'

'You've got an amazing act.'

'Not according to some people on Twitter. They think it would be much fairer if I was put in a special category for disabled performers.'

'They stink.'

'I so agree. But if I let them get to me they've won. That's why I'll never hide myself away and not answer my phone.'

'Unlike me, I suppose,' I said. 'Maddy thinks I've been acting like a great big baby. And I'm just guessing here that you agree with her.'

'Totally.'

'So do I, now. And did you just ring to have a go at me?'

'Yes, I mean no, of course I didn't. I'm rehearsing my show today and recording it tomorrow. I'm allowed one guest tomorrow to do a three-minute spot. And do you know who I've picked?'

I hardly dared answer. I hardly dared even breathe.

'It sounds insane, but I picked you. Because' – her voice softened a little – 'you helped me when I most needed it. I might have wheeled myself off *Kids with Attitude* if it hadn't been for you and also, you're so annoyingly good. Well, say something.'

'Poppy, ever since you won I've been sticking pins in your picture. But now, as a mark of my gratitude I'm going to stop.'

She laughed. 'Now you sound like Louis again.'

'Now I feel like Louis again. Thank you! And I'll never forget what you've done for me—'

'No time for that,' she interrupted. 'I've pretended to everyone that you know all the details already, so here they are.' She rattled them off and then had to tear away for a sound check or something and I looked at Maddy. 'Did you know?'

'I sort of guessed, hoped.'

'I can't believe it.'

'Nor can I,' she agreed.

'And if you hadn't stopped me getting on that train – well, fire's only just been invented where my grandparents live. And I'd have missed the greatest chance of my life. So what do we do now?'

'Go back to school,' said Maddy a bit doubtfully.

'Well, I certainly don't want to be in any more trouble. As it is I'll have to explain why I've missed the morning, and am turning up with a bag containing not one school book? But I can't go back, just yet. Not after that news. We must have a little celebration first.'

Maddy agreed. 'But we can't go anywhere too conspicuous, just in case one of our teachers is roaming about.'

'Yeah, can you imagine if I saw Beachy Head now? Tell you what, there's a little café just by the station. It's a bit dead, but no one will see us there.'

'Come on, then,' said Maddy.

As we walked over to it we glanced idly in the window. It was practically deserted. So I could ask Maddy here if she really was going out with Edgar. But then Maddy let out a cry of horror. 'Look away.'

'Why?'

'Do you know who's sitting in there?'

'Tell me it's not Beachy Head.'

'It's not Beachy Head. It's worse.'

'Worse than Beachy Head,' I began. 'That's not possible.' And then I murmured, 'Oh yes it is.' For I'd sneaked a look and spotted my dad. I couldn't believe it. 'But he's off to London to see some business colleagues.'

'Perhaps he's having a coffee first,' said Maddy.

'I'm sure he said he had to be in London for nine o'clock.'

I glanced again at Dad, hunched away in the darkest corner. He seemed bowed down with shame. 'No, Maddy,' I said, 'my poor old dad is leading a double life. He's pretending he's got all these high-powered meetings, when really he's skulking about in here.'

'That's so sad,' said Maddy. 'Best if we just pretend we haven't seen him.'

'Yeah,' I agreed. 'He wouldn't want us uncovering his secret. And I don't want to have to explain why we're here.'

'No,' she agreed. 'Come on, then.'

But I couldn't resist taking one last glance at Dad.

And that's when he looked up and stared right back at me.

Chapter Twenty-Two
Dad's Double Life

11.50 p.m.

Dad's face totally froze. It was as if I'd just hit the pause button. He couldn't believe I was outside the window.

So how about if I just stole away? Maybe then Dad would figure his peepers had been playing tricks and I was only – what do you call it ...? Yeah, a mirage. Dead-thirsty people get them in deserts, don't they? Just a shame Dad wasn't in a desert right now. He wasn't exactly thirsty either – not with a massive coffee right by him.

Then all at once it was as if play had been pressed again and Dad came to life, looking incredibly shocked and kind of embarrassed too. He was also standing up and beckoning me inside.

'I'll leave you,' said Maddy.

'Don't you dare, there's safety in numbers,' I replied. I was sweating buckets but tried to saunter over to Dad in a carefree manner. He was still standing up. 'Howdy, Dad, great to see you.'

'Is it?' he replied very dryly. 'Sit down.' The chairs were big and heavy and Maddy and I clambered down opposite him.

'Never been in here before,' I went on chattily. 'Would you recommend it? I'll have a coffee if you're paying.'

'Why aren't you in school?' demanded Dad.

'Would you believe I got lost,' I said, not very hopefully. 'I thought I was on my way to school and ended up here. It's probably the after-effects of my bug. I read somewhere it can cause temporary loss of memory.'

'Think again,' said Dad.

I glanced at Maddy and she nodded her head very slightly. I knew what message she was sending – tell him the truth.

'This'll make you laugh,' I said to Dad. 'I was running away, but I'm not now because I've had some news.'

'Totally awesome news,' cut in Maddy.

202

'Yeah, just wait until you hear—'

But Dad was still thinking about the other thing I'd said. 'You were running away?'

'Afraid so,' I admitted.

'But where to?'

'To Nan and Grandad in the country. I thought I could start a new life there. Not permanently, only for a year or so. And I'd arrange for you and Mum to come and visit, of course.'

'And do your grandparents know about this?' asked Dad.

'No, it was a sort of early Christmas present for them.'

'So you two,' said Dad, speaking slowly and deliberately, 'were going to just turn up on their doorstep? I must say, Maddy, I'm surprised at you.'

'Oh no, Maddy wasn't going to live with my grandparents,' I said. 'Maddy's only here because she's been watching our house.'

Now Dad looked more confused than ever.

'I mean, she's only been watching it since this morning.' I turned to her. 'You thought I might run away, didn't you?'

'I so did,' said Maddy.

'But why did you want to run away, Louis?' Dad asked quietly.

'Well, look, it was nothing you've done,' I said

at once, 'or Mum. It was …' How on earth could I explain it?

'The pressure of fame really, wasn't it?' prompted Maddy.

'That's it, exactly,' I said. 'Everyone looking at me and thinking I'm a total freak because I threw up on live telly. I just didn't feel like me any more. So I thought I'd escape it all. And I was queuing up for my ticket when my probation officer here' – I grinned at Maddy – 'turned up and had a right go at me.'

'Good for you, Maddy,' said Dad. Then he fixed his gaze on me. 'I'm glad you didn't take the easy way out.' He looked thoughtful for a moment.

Here it comes, I said to myself – the big lecture. I knew all the signs.

But instead Dad said very unexpectedly, 'I imagine you were surprised to see me in here.'

'Er, just a bit,' I replied cautiously.

'You were probably wondering why I wasn't in London.'

'Not really,' I said brightly. 'I expect your meeting got delayed, didn't it?' I was trying to help him out here.

So was Maddy, who added, 'My dad's meetings are always being changed.'

'No, I told a white lie,' Dad said. 'I didn't

have a meeting in London and I shouldn't have pretended. Don't know why I did that, bit embarrassed, I suppose, because ...' Dad's face had turned incredibly red. 'Well, on the Internet recently I've been talking to someone. And that's who I'm meeting here now.'

Maddy leaped from her chair as if it had suddenly become red hot. 'I must go,' she cried.

While I wondered what on earth was Dad about to tell me? Well, whatever it was I was too young to hear it. I wanted a dad who wore bulky sweaters and got furious about the price of potatoes. Not this new dodgy version skulking about in greasy spoons meeting people off the Internet.

'Please sit down, Maddy,' said Dad quietly. 'I don't want any more secrets, so I want you both to know. I'm meeting' – I actually closed my eyes here – 'someone who runs a small support group for stay-at-home dads. He and another guy from the group are coming here now ...'

That's when Maddy and I let out the most massive sigh of relief you've ever heard.

'They will help me learn some new skills and make some new contacts too,' said Dad. Plus, they also run a small course for dads on cooking.'

'But will a small course be enough, Dad?' I teased.

He grinned. 'I thought you and Elliot needed a break from beans on toast and omelettes.'

'Too right,' I said. 'If Mum hadn't added some stuff every night I'd be eating my hands now.'

'Well, that's all going to change. I shall soon be serving such culinary delights ...' Suddenly Dad stood up, 'Actually, I really think this might be my guests now.'

It was. Two very cheerful-looking guys shook hands with Dad while I whispered to Maddy, 'But they look ... normal.' Then I quickly went on, 'Why did I say that? Why shouldn't they be normal?'

'Because people are always trying to put other people in little boxes,' she replied fiercely. 'Only women are allowed to be at home all day. And I think that's so lazy and stupid because it stops people being everything they could be, and—'

'Maddy, calm down,' I interrupted. 'I agree with you.'

Then Dad came speeding back. He'd explained to the two guys that he had to quickly whisk us off to school. So he dropped Maddy off at her school first. As she was leaving, she hissed, 'Don't forget to tell your dad the good news.'

How could I have forgotten that? So I did tell Dad. He was dead chuffed but then said, 'In the café you said you were running away because you didn't feel like yourself …'

I nodded a bit cautiously.

'Well, I haven't felt like myself for a while either.'

'Since you lost your job.'

'Yeah, it was as if something had gone missing – the most important part of me.' He gave a low chuckle. 'That's why I think I enjoyed doing your homework so much.'

'Any time,' I murmured.

'I enjoyed your company too, Louis.'

'I can understand that.'

'So much, in fact, there were times when I forgot I'm also your dad. I shouldn't have done that. Only confuses things. Sorry.'

One of my parents was actually apologizing to me!

But then he spoilt it all by announcing, 'By the way, we've arranged for you to have a tutor.'

I could only stare at him in undisguised horror.

'Want to know who it is – it's me?'

'Actually, Dad, I think I preferred our old arrangement, where you just did my homework.'

'Sorry, not on offer.'

'Well then, I should warn you,' I said, 'I'm incapable of concentrating on schoolwork for more than two seconds. I mean, I make goldfish look intellectual. But I suppose you can have a go if you like.'

Then Dad said softly, 'I will *get* another job, you know.'

'I know you will,' I replied at once. 'But actually, I think it's cool you and Mum have swapped about – I suppose you're sort of rebels really. I'm even proud of you. Well, I will be when you can cook something other than beans on toast.'

Chapter Twenty-Three
Intergalactic at Least

7.50 p.m.

Tonight Dad told Mum and Elliot he's joined this stay-at-home dads support group and has signed up for their cookery course. 'That was actually the business meeting I had today,' he admitted, looking a bit sheepish.

Then he told Mum about seeing me at the café this morning, and why I'd been there. And I stood waiting for a massive rollicking, but she said, 'Sometimes, Louis, we all feel like running away and I can see why you did.'

'Can you really?' I asked. I was astonished.

'Oh yes – but I'm very, very glad you came home.'

And that was all. No massive rollicking. Incredible.

9.30 p.m.
A man goes into a pet shop and says he wants to buy a wasp. The pet shop owner says he doesn't sell wasps.

'Yes you do,' the man replies. 'There's one in the window.'

Another one:

Why can't the skeleton go to the disco?
Because it has no body to dance with.

Oh yeah, the jokes are pouring out of me now. But when I first performed my act for Maddy today I'd actually gone a bit dry. I've only stopped being a comedian for a few days, but already my comedy levels had declined dramatically. Can you believe that?

Friday December 20th

6.50 a.m.
Been awake for ages already. And even though my bedroom is colder than Siberia I've been walking about practising my comedy act.

210

There won't be a car to take us to the studio today – we've got to find our own way there. So we're getting the train. Luckily it's the last day of term and school finishes at half past twelve. So we should arrive there easily for five o'clock.

And it's not only Dad and Maddy travelling with me this time. Mum's given herself the afternoon off (well, she is practically the boss now), and Little Legs will be there too.

By the way, I'm not telling anyone at school I'm doing this, just in case – well, just in case.

5.00 p.m.
The second I arrived at the TV Studios the shame of my last appearance came roaring back. I didn't think anyone had noticed, but then Maddy whispered, 'Never forget you're a different person tonight.'

It was her idea to give me a whole new look. So I've gone smart – with a suit, bow tie, shiniest shoes you've ever seen, and for a bit of razzle dazzle a very red waistcoat which Maddy found in a charity shop. I'm not altogether surprised it was chucked out – it is incredibly bright – but if this get-up doesn't wipe out 'Vomit Boy' nothing will.

5.25 p.m.
Evie was waiting for us. I said cheerily to her, 'I bet you never expected to see me again. Sorry for being so spectacularly disgusting last time.'

'Well, you were naughty,' said Evie, 'not telling us how ill you were. But you wanted your chance. And the show certainly had a lot of publicity ...' She hesitated.

'After I gobbed all over the presenter,' I interrupted. 'Don't worry, I'll be on my best behaviour tonight.'

5.40 p.m.
Maddy and my family are in the studio theatre now. I've had a bit of make-up flung on me. So, not long now.

5.56 p.m.
Poppy dropped by.

I said, 'Look, if I don't say it later, thanks again for ...'

'The budget for this show was so small we couldn't get anyone else,' she grinned. 'So go out there and be great – but not too great. Remember whose show it is.'

'Yeah, sure – what's your name again?'

Evie sped in then. Poppy was needed urgently. So she had to go, and I had another little pang of envy. It must be great to be needed urgently. But still, I was here. And that was incredible.

Then Evie came back and said this show was being recorded, so it didn't matter if I made a mistake. But they'd still rather I didn't, as time was very tight.

And I will be on soon. Straight after Poppy has introduced her show and done a brief opening magic trick, in fact.

Amazing, really, that just two days ago I was getting ready to run away. Wednesday feels like months ago now and – hey, I think I can hear something.

Yes, I can.

Evie's high heels are tripping along the corridor. She's come to fetch me, hasn't she?

A jolt of panic shoots through me. But no, I mustn't get scared: this is what I've dreamed of, what I've waited so long for.

And I won't mess it up this time.

I WON'T.

9.20 p.m.

It was over insanely fast. The three minutes just went in a flash. And I could have stayed out there so much longer. I wasn't nervous either. Not when I was actually out on the stage.

Anyway, afterwards the audience clapped

away and Poppy gave me the thumbs up before wheeling herself back onto the stage. Then Evie whispered that I wouldn't need to re-do it, and a girl I'd never seen before escorted me to the Green Room, where she said my family would be waiting.

But they must have taken longer getting out of the theatre than expected. For at first the Green Room was completely empty. Talk about an anti-climax.

Finally, my family surged in, but then they all stopped talking when they saw me. For a couple of seconds there, everyone just gaped at me.

Talk about unnerving. Had something gone wrong? Something I hadn't noticed. With me, that was very likely. But then they all just erupted into mad cheering and there was this hubbub of voices, with Mum shouting, 'You were sensational, Louis!'

Now 'sensational' is not a word my mum uses very often and never in connection with me! Then Dad said, 'Hands down, your best ever performance, I couldn't be prouder.'

'Neither could I,' said Mum.

'I suppose I'm a bit proud too,' chipped in Elliot.

Then Dad and Mum went on about how they were going to tell everyone when I was on the telly. (Christmas Eve, 5 p.m.) They really were bursting with it all.

As for Maddy, she smiled quite shyly at me and said, 'Tonight it was as if I'd never seen you before. When this goes out, you're going to be … intergalactic, at least.'

We hung about in the Green Room for a bit, thinking Evie or someone from the TV Company would burst in and say, 'Well done' or 'Happy Christmas,' but I guess they were all too busy. So in the end we all just slunk off. But I tell you, nothing could take the shine off tonight. In fact, if a trail of light had followed me as I soared down the corridor I really wouldn't have been very surprised.

9.35 p.m.
I've saved until, last, dear Diary, the most important news.

Maddy came back to my house for a bit. But we hardly got a chance to chat as Elliot, now feeling a bit left out of it all, insisted on acting out his entire part from *Oliver*. And we all had to sit and applaud him wildly.

But just before she left, Maddy and I were on our own in the kitchen. That's when she said to me, all in a rush, 'By the way, I'm not going out with Edgar. He only said that to you to get a reaction.'

My hopes rose.

'And I won't ever go out on a date with you again either.'

Only to be totally dashed again. Talk about ending a top evening on a downer.

She sped on. 'There are some things I just can't do, such as talk in public, act in public, have anything to do with rats or snakes … or go on dates – with anyone. Well, our last date was a disaster, wasn't it?'

Before I could reply she said, 'I knew it would be when I had my hair done specially. It was supposed to be tight curls, but the curls started uncurling before we left the hairdresser's. And soon I looked like snot on legs.'

'Maddy, you so didn't.'

'Louis, will you do me a favour?'

'Anything.'

'Shut up interrupting and let me finish what I want to say.'

'Sorry.'

'The thing is, I'll never go on a date ever again – not in my whole life. But I will go on an *un*date – with one person – you.'

'An undate,' I repeated, and then thought about it for a moment. 'So we'd go to say, the cinema together, but not tell anyone it's a date.'

'Not even ourselves,' said Maddy.

'And there'd be no dressing up, or doing our hair.'

'Definitely no doing our hair,' said Maddy.

Grinning now, I put my hand on hers and asked, 'Maddy, would you like to go on an undate with me?'

'More than anything in the world,' she said.

So that's brilliant news. The best. The only problem is, I'm *not* sure when we'll have that undate yet, as – and you're not going to believe this – I'm still grounded until the New Year. But don't worry, I'm going to work on my parents and rattle on about the spirit of Christmas.

Anyway, I do know exactly where Maddy will be on Christmas Eve at 5 p.m. She'll be round my house with Mum, Dad, Elliot and yours truly, watching me on Poppy's show.

I'm only on for three minutes (hope they don't cut it) but still I'll be there on the telly, telling jokes. I've moved closer to my dream. So, never give up hope, OK? Just keep on battling away and ...

But there's no space to tell you any more as I'm right at the end of another diary. Can you believe that?

You've been such a top audience. I want to leave you with one last joke. It's dead silly, so

217

one of my favourites.

What do you call a magician from outer space?
   A flying sorcerer.

Smile on and on and on.
   Louis the Laugh

Coming soon!

Louis the Laugh's
hilarious adventures
continue in...

HOW TO UPDATE YOUR PARENTS

ISBN 978-1-78270-172-9

My mum and dad have terrible ideas. In fact, it's their main hobby.

BUT THIS IS THEIR WORST IDEA EVER.

They moan about the amount of time I spend 'glued to screens' but I never for a moment, guessed – well just listen to this...

Whenever I'm at home **THEY ARE BANNING ME FROM USING COMPUTERS, LAPTOPS, iPADS AND PHONES** – in fact, anything that shows I'm living in the 21st century.

At first I thought it was just a terrible joke. And then – **WELL THE SHOCK HAS PROBABLY DAMAGED ME FOR LIFE.**

But they keep saying how we're going to have **"EXCELLENT FUN"** playing board games, going for long walks and communicating with each other again.

JUST KILL ME NOW.

I've got to stop this mad scheme, haven't I? **BUT HOW?**

Maddy thinks she has the solution...

Pete Johnson Facts

Pete's favourite subjects at school were English and History. His least favourite was Maths.

He has two dogs – a West Highland terrier called Hattie and a King Charles Spaniel named Tilly.

Pete has always loved reading. When he was younger he would read up to six books a week – even more in the school holidays!

His most favourite book as a child was *One Hundred and One Dalmatians*. He wrote to the author, Dodie Smith, and she encouraged him to become a writer.

Other childhood favourites include *The Witches* by Roald Dahl, *Tom's Midnight Garden* by Philippa Pearce and Enid Blyton's *The Mystery of the Invisible Thief*.

When he was younger, Pete used to sleepwalk. One night he woke up in his pyjamas walking along a busy road.

His favourite food is chocolate. He especially loves Easter eggs!

He loved to watch old black and white movies with his dad on Saturday night and used to review films on Radio 1. Sometimes he watched three films in a day! Pete has met lots of famous actors and collects signed film pictures.

Pete likes to start writing by eight o'clock in the morning. He reads all his books out loud to see if the dialogue sounds right. And if he's stuck for an idea he goes for a long walk.

Wherever he goes, Pete always carries a notebook with him. The best ideas come when you're least expecting them, he says. Why don't you try that too? Maybe you'll have a brilliant idea for your own book!

Louis's Joke Book

Here are some of Louis's favourite jokes...

What do you get when you cross an angry bee
with a giant ape?
Sting Kong.

What is the fastest part of a car?
The dashboard.

What do you call a donkey with three legs?
A wonky.

Why did the coach throw Cinderella off the
football team?
Because she ran away from the ball.

What did the ghost teacher say to the class?
Look at the board and I'll go through it again.

Teacher: What can you tell me about
the Dead Sea?
Pupil: I didn't know it was sick.

Smile on!